D1488099

TEN OF SWORDS

Also by J. R. Levitt

Carnivores

J.R. LEVITT

TEN

OF

SWORDS

A THOMAS DUNNE BOOK

St. Martin's Press
New York

TEN OF SWORDS. Copyright © 1991 by J. R. Levitt. All rights reserved. Printed in the United States of America. No part of this book may be used or reproduced in any manner whatsoever without written permission except in the case of brief quotations embodied in critical articles or reviews. For information, address St. Martin's Press, 175 Fifth Avenue, New York, N.Y. 10010.

Design by Dawn Niles

Library of Congress Cataloging-in-Publication Data

Levitt, J. R.
    Ten of swords / J.R. Levitt.
        p.   cm.
    "A Thomas Dunne book."
    ISBN 0-312-05386-X
    I. Title.
PS3562.E9223T4   1991
813'.54—dc20   90-49314
                                                                   CIP

First Edition: February 1991

10 9 8 7 6 5 4 3 2 1

TEN OF SWORDS

1

Marie Gasteau leaned across the coffee table between us and took my hand. Too much perfume wafted toward me. Too much eye shadow stared at me. Too much lipstick surrounded the words coming out of her mouth.

"How long will it take to find Monica, Mr. Coulter?" she asked.

"That's Jason," I said. "It depends. She might not even be in Salt Lake, you know."

She examined me, looking dubiously at my hair, which had grown a bit shaggy lately. I was wearing a dark short-sleeved shirt and gray jeans. I obviously didn't fit her image of a private investigator. She reached up unconsciously and fluffed her own hair, bright orange, tightly curled. She wore mother of pearl earrings the size of earmuffs. Fifty, trying to look thirty-five, and not succeeding.

"Oh, she's here somewhere. She's done this before, but never for so long. And last time, she was living with some nigger. I told the police that, but they didn't seem very interested." She pursed her lips and sniffed. "I guess a sixteen-year-old girl in trouble just isn't that important."

2

Her husband interrupted. He hadn't said much up to now, just sat on the couch next to his wife, listening. He had ears that stuck out and nervous hands.

"They have a lot of runaways, dear," he said mildly.

I looked down at the coffee table between us. Magazines were arranged in a fan, covers barely overlapping. The wallpaper in the room was pink and perfect. The rug was chocolate brown and deep and freshly vacuumed. The pictures on the wall were bland and razor straight. The type of home you might well want to run away from. But there are an awful lot of things that can happen to a runaway girl, even in Salt Lake. Rape. Murder. Things like that. Marie leaned over and handed me a snapshot.

"Monica," she said.

A teenage girl with dark shoulder-length hair, maybe five-four or so, quite pretty, lounged against a dead tree. She looked bored.

"Where does she go to school?" I asked.

Marie hesitated. "Go on, tell him," said her husband.

She sniffed again. "She was going to Skyline, but she got thrown out. Some trouble with a teacher."

The husband interrupted. "Her English teacher. He claimed she was trying to blackmail him. Monica said they were having an affair."

"What happened to the teacher?" I asked.

"Oh, they fired him," Marie said. "Pervert."

"And the doctor," her husband said. "Don't forget about the doctor."

I waited, but he didn't say anything else. I asked a few questions—friends, interests, stuff like that—and took the snapshot with me.

I got started looking for Monica the next day. If you're searching a city for a missing girl, especially in nice weather, a good place to look is in a park. Parks are all different—some cater to families with children, some to joggers, some end up with speed freaks and burnouts. But if the park is large enough, or in the right place, sooner or later everyone passes through.

In Salt Lake City the place to go on a Sunday afternoon is Liberty Park. It's close enough to walk to from downtown. There's a pool, a playground, an aviary with exotic birds, concession stands, spreading shade trees to block the summer sun, and even a small lake.

It's not a big park, considering how many people use it, maybe half a mile long and a quarter mile wide, but each section of the park is like a little island. The different groups stake out a particular section of turf, casting unfriendly eyes upon the occasional intruder.

It was crowded for an October Sunday. I'd been through it a half dozen times since noon without any luck. I walked around the asphalt loop where lowriders cruise and joggers jog, dodging Lycra-covered skaters as they weaved through the crowded center strip on their polyethylene wheels. I ambled through where picnickers spread their tablecloths on the cool grass. I watched as lemonade was sipped and drugs were sold and lovers strolled casually among the trees. But no Monica.

I didn't really think it was going to be that easy, just running across her in the park. But Salt Lake isn't a very big city, as cities go, and the places where teenage kids like to hang out are pretty standard. A couple of the arcades, Crossroads Mall, Washington Square Park, Memory Grove, State Street if they're hooking. And of course, Liberty Park. I had to start somewhere.

By six P.M. I was bored. That's what being a PI is all about, but it's not as if I had a lot of choice. When you're an ex-cop, especially a homicide cop, there's really not a whole lot else you can do. Most companies won't hire guys in their thirties unless they have experience, and the type of experience I had doesn't translate well into other fields. "So, Mr. Coulter, you know a lot about dead people? And you're reasonably proficient with a firearm? And you occasionally have been known to lean on people? Why, you're just perfect for us!" You bet.

I sat down under a catalpa tree by the north entrance, still holding on to the faint hope that Monica would just saunter by. I lit up a Pall Mall and leaned back against my tree, appreciating a blonde on roller skates darting in and out of the crowd. It was just starting to get dark. Two jogging couples cruised by on their third pass around the loop—two boys about eighteen, both black, and two white girls a little younger. I had been paying attention to the girls, since one of them looked a lot like the snapshot of Monica I was carrying, but when they passed by close on their third circuit I could see it wasn't her.

I ground out the cigarette against the heel of my shoe and got to my feet. One more pass through the park wouldn't hurt. I had been sitting cross-legged under the tree and my knees protested as I straightened up. Another cheerful reminder that I wasn't as young as I used to be. I strolled off toward the southwest corner of the loop, and as I passed through I got a few chilly looks, not actively hostile, but not exactly friendly either. Mostly Chicanos hang out there, and Anglos are not particularly welcome. Except for cute teenage girls. Cute teenage girls are always welcome.

The local cholos sprawled on the grass and stared contemptuously, drinking beer, smoking weed. One of them called out something in Spanish at me, and the others all laughed. The older Chicanos, those with families of their own, looked at the cholos with disapproval. The men glowered with anger. The women shook their heads sadly and turned away.

No sign of Monica. I angled across the park to the southeast corner, filled each afternoon with car freaks of all sorts, drawn together by their common interest, incessantly polishing their automobiles to gleaming perfection. No Monica. I didn't bother to check the northeast corner. That's the province of young Mormon couples, mostly white, mostly plump, mostly with small children, very sedate.

I cut back to the center strip that runs the length of the park. It's closed to traffic and crowded with equal numbers of young blacks and whites listening to ghetto blasters, talking trash, just hanging out. I'd spent most of the day earlier talking to the street kids there. A lot of them knew Monica. Most liked her; a few didn't. The ones who liked her wouldn't talk to me. The ones who didn't were a lot more help, since they figured she must be in trouble and were eager for a chance to rat her off. But after separating out the lies and bullshit, it was becoming clear that no one had seen her for quite a while.

I ended up back underneath my tree. I sighed. It looked like just hanging around the park wasn't going to pan out. Finding Monica was going to take some actual work after all.

I sat idly for a while, watching the passing show. The jogging couples came around the loop again. One of the boys was tall and very dark, close-cropped hair shaved on the sides, good-looking. The other was shorter and lighter skinned. They both had on jogging outfits and Reeboks, and moved easily, like serious athletes. They carried themselves as though they knew what they were doing and wanted to make sure everyone else knew that they knew it. The girls were another story. The dark-haired one, the one who looked like Monica, was wearing red plastic sandals, of all things, and matching red shorts. She looked like she knew what she was doing, too, and it didn't have anything to do with running. The other, a thin, pale-complexioned girl with long brown hair pinned up, had on a pair of old-fashioned tennis shoes. Another serious jogger. She kept begging the boys to take it easy. The boys looked properly disdainful.

They were having a good time, though, the boys running ahead, slowing down to let the girls catch up, running ahead again, talking and giggling. They stopped across the

6

loop from me. The girls plopped themselves down on the grass while the boys did stretching exercises.

The taller boy waved at someone, and another young girl joined them from across the park. I sat up and squinted toward them. The distance was a bit too far for me to be positive, but she sure looked a lot like the picture of Monica I was carrying. Maybe it was going to be just that easy after all.

I got up and casually headed in their direction as they jogged slowly out of the park, with the one who looked like Monica lagging behind. The rest started across the intersection, walking now side by side, boy-girl, boy-girl, crossing with the light. The shorter boy was talking to the girls, serious for the moment. The taller began dancing around, circling the others, turning sideways, walking backward, just goofing. A bunch of kids having fun.

Then I heard it. A flat, cracking sound, not nearly as loud as a car backfire, but far more ominous. The tall boy stopped, motionless, looking at an arm suddenly useless hanging at his side. It was covered with blood. The girl I thought was Monica was already running, halfway to Seventh East. The other dark girl screamed and the boy pushed at her with his good arm, shouting, "Run, Sandy!" The girls took off back through the park, and as they scattered, more shots started coming, measured and even but fast. The tall boy was hit again, this time in the shoulder, spinning him around, then again, in the back. The shorter boy jumped over to him and tried to help, grabbing him under the arms in a bear hug, pulling him toward the curb. The tall boy was hit in the back again, and this time the round passed right through his body, and through the shorter boy as well. The shooter was using a high-powered rifle.

Both kids were on the ground now. The tall boy wasn't moving, but the other was trying to crawl away. He dragged himself toward the only available cover, an overgrown field full of weeds and rubble directly west of the intersection. Unfortunately, that was precisely where the shooter was hiding. He got hit twice more. It looked like the hits were from head on, through the top of the left shoulder, then the right shoulder. I could see his body jerk each time. The way he was hit, he probably didn't have a single internal organ left intact.

There was a moment of silence that stretched out until I realized it was over. The whole thing had taken maybe twelve seconds. I ran toward the boys, zigzagging, trying to keep one of the trees between me and that deadly field across the intersection. I heard the roar of an engine across the street and saw a late model Firebird or Camaro pull out from the far side of the field. I couldn't get a plate in the dusk. I couldn't even get a color, except that it was something dark.

The park turned into a circus, people yelling advice, others just shouting and running, mostly away from the area. I could hear the sound of a paramedic ambulance siren in the distance. A young woman in a nursing outfit ran into the intersection to try to help the two boys. She hadn't seen the car leave, and for all she knew, the guy was reloading for a second round of sniping. She had guts. Another guy pulled his pickup across the intersection, trying to shield the two kids. He parked on the wrong side of them. It didn't matter anyway. It was too late for anyone to help.

I reached the first kid with some vague idea of starting CPR, but there wasn't any point. Handguns are bad enough, but rifles are destroyers. A round from a high-powered rifle striking the shoulder can tear an arm right off. The shock and blood loss alone can sometimes kill you. If I wanted to start CPR on him I had a problem. There wasn't much of anything left of his chest to push on. He was gutted like a deer.

The paramedic truck pulled in so fast I had to jump out of the way to keep from getting run down. As it was, they almost ran over the boy at my feet. The paramedics

8

jumped out of the truck, bent over him, saw what I'd seen, and left him lying there.

The other kid wasn't a whole lot better, but at least he was intact. Incredibly, he was still breathing, barely, with a choking, gurgling sound. The rest of the paramedic crew gathered around the boy and dutifully started working on him, trying for a save. It wasn't going to happen, though, and I could see they knew it.

The cops started arriving a minute later, uniformed cars from all over the East Side. I walked away. There wasn't anything I could do. The first two cops on the scene were a couple of rookies I didn't know. They looked nervous as hell, but at least they knew enough about procedure to clear away the crowd from where the two kids were lying. "Protect the scene" is what's drilled into every cop who goes through the academy. "Preserve the evidence." They were so concerned with clearing away the crowd they hardly even glanced at the two bodies in the street. If they'd dared, they would have kept the paramedics out as well. Both cops cast desperately around for a convenient location to herd the crowd to, and they quickly came up with the most logical spot: the overgrown field across the intersection. They didn't realize that the field was the real scene, the important scene, not where the kids had fallen. The field was where the shooter had parked his car and fired his rifle. The field was where the killer would have left his traces. And in two minutes there were going to be a hundred people trampling that field flat.

It wasn't any of my business, but old habits die hard. I walked up to the one who seemed to be taking charge and said, "Sorry to butt in, but that field you're pushing people into is where the shots came from."

He glanced at me with that contemptuous arrogance for civilians that only a rookie cop can muster. His uniform was crisp and new and clean. "Yeah?" he said, continuing to wave them toward the field. "And just who might you be?"

"My name's Coulter," I said. "Jason Coulter. I used to work Homicide." He gave me a quick glance which told me the name had registered.

"Yeah, so I've heard." He kept on waving in the crowd, showing me that ex-cops didn't impress him any. "Well, you don't work it anymore, do you?"

I shrugged and walked away, wondering if he was typical of what they were hiring these days. The homicide squad was going to have a fit when they found that the evidence was screwed.

It took about half an hour for anyone from Homicide to get there. It was Mike Volter. I used to work for Mike. I was surprised because sergeants don't usually get to things until most of the mess is cleared up. He'd put on a few pounds since I'd seen him last, and he wasn't exactly svelte to begin with. He wasn't a bad cop. Just not a whole lot of imagination. He'd never liked me much when I worked for him and he liked me a lot less now.

The paramedics rushed the one kid off to the hospital, where he was going to be DOA. The other was still lying forlornly in the street, waiting for the crime lab and the M.E. On the grass at the edge of the park the pale girl was sitting on the ground sobbing, her friend next to her. One of the paramedics was tending to her. Her leg was bloody, but it didn't look bad enough to be a direct hit. Maybe a fragment from a ricochet. There was no sign of the girl who looked like Monica.

I waited until Volter had finished talking to the uniformed cops and came up behind him. One of the uniforms tried to herd me off but stopped when he saw that the sergeant knew me.

"Hello, Mike." I said. "Quite a mess, huh?"

He looked over his shoulder. "Jason Coulter," he said. "Well, well, well."

"Good to see you too, Mike."

"You got some reason to be here, Jason?"

10

"Just sitting in the park minding my business. Then all hell broke loose."

"Yeah. I noticed."

"Thought I'd offer some free advice."

"Don't bother," he said.

I ignored him. "You want to know where the shots came from?"

Mike looked at me, considering. "Where?"

I pointed at the field, now almost solidly packed with curious gawkers. Mike looked over at the crowd, then back at me. "Oh, Christ," he said. I nodded agreement.

"Fairly light-caliber rifle, from the sound. The way the shots were spaced, I'd say probably a bolt action."

Mike wasn't paying attention. He was headed over toward the field, pulling a couple of uniformed cops with him. The rookie I had originally talked to was one of them. Mike had his face right up close to his, and neither one of them looked happy. The rookie glanced back at me. I gave him a cheery wave.

They started moving people out of the field. The crime lab van drove up, and Jerry Archibald got out and looked around vaguely. Jerry was one of the few real old-timers left. Five silver service stars rode over the pocket of his uniform shirt. He wasn't overly swift, though. Mike motioned him over toward the field.

I waited around to see if Dave Warren would show up. I hadn't seen Dave in quite a while. Dave also worked Homicide, my ex-partner from back when. After I left the department, we hadn't talked at all for a few months. He was too much a part of what had happened. But gradually, the strain between us had eased. I doubted we'd ever get back the free and easy way we'd once had, but we were friends again, or something close to it. I didn't see him arrive, but his New York accent pronouncing my name behind me made me turn my head.

"Jason. What's going on, buddy?"

"Damned if I know," I said. "Someone started shooting, and people started dying."

"You see it?"

"I'm afraid so," I said, running it down for him the best I could.

"Wait a minute," Dave interrupted. "Where did you say the shots were coming from?"

I pointed at the field again, still half full. Dave shook his head. "And there was a car?"

"Right near the back."

Dave looked over at the people milling around in the field and sighed. "Well, let's take a look," he said.

We walked over to the crime lab van and grabbed Jerry. It was almost full dark by now, but Jerry had one of those super-high-intensity cadmium battery flashlights with him. He flashed it around the area I pointed out. The ground was scuffed up, with broken bottles and flattened cans scattered through the weeds. It looked pretty unpromising. He played the flash back and forth until I said, "There," and stopped the light.

"What?" he asked.

"Right there. The tire track." Amazingly, there was still about six inches of tire tread untrampled in the soft earth near the back.

Dave walked over and squatted down next to the track, careful not to touch it. "Can we get a cast of this?" he asked. Jerry bent over and looked at it closely.

"It'll be difficult," he said morosely.

"How come?"

Jerry gestured toward the track. "Look at it. This bit here is nice and clear, sure. I can get a good photo of it. But it's in a real fine, powdery dust, see? The minute you drop wet plaster onto it for a cast, you're just going to wipe the pattern out completely. All you'll get is a blur."

"How about silicone spray?" Dave asked. "Can you use silicone spray?"

12

"I could if I had any. We ran out."

"You ran out."

Jerry stared at him, half belligerent, half defensive. "Yeah. We ran out."

"Worthless motherfucker," Dave muttered, just loud enough for me to hear. I looked over at the 7-Eleven across the street. "How about hair spray?" I asked.

"Hair spray?" Jerry wasn't real quick about handling a new thought.

"Yeah, sure," Dave said, picking up on it right away. "Get some hair spray from the 7-Eleven and spray it lightly over the track. Let it dry, spray it again. Keep doing that until it's stiff enough to hold a cast."

Jerry regarded him at length, not enthusiastic. "Might work," he finally admitted.

"Well?"

"Well what?"

"Well, why the fuck don't you get a can and see if it does," Dave said, pointing at the store.

Jerry's eyes followed Dave's finger. He stood there for a minute, apparently lost in thought. "Sure," he said at last. "Why not?" He looked back at Dave, and then at me. "Either of you got a couple of bucks?"

Some things never change.

2

I slept late and got up just in time to catch the news at noon on TV. The jogger murders were the lead story. Usually a couple of murders are worth just a brief mention, but this was different. First, these were two young kids. Second, these were two young black kids, and already there was speculation whether it might not be some sort of racial vendetta.

There was a background story on the kids. One of them, Bill Daniels, was on a football scholarship at the University of Utah. They interviewed one of the assistant football coaches. He said it was a tragedy and a terrific blow to the team's chances this fall. As an afterthought, he added what a great guy Bill had been. The other was identified as Isaac Tremayne, a student at East High.

There also was an interview with Captain Riggs, head of the detective division. I expected the usual bullshit about following up promising leads, but it didn't come off that way. Riggs didn't say anything specific; he was too cagey for that. You don't make Captain by shooting your mouth off to the press. But I could tell by the smirk on his face that he thought they were on to something. He was just dying to tell the reporter the case was about to be broken. I wondered what they'd come up with.

About one-thirty, Dave called, and we went through the usual pleasantries.

"So what's going on with these two black kids?" I finally asked. "Riggs looked like he was about to give birth right on TV."

"That asshole. As soon as he thought we had it sewed up he did his little dance and shuffle for the press."

"And now it's not so tight?"

"It's a mess. Meet me for a cup?"

"Sure. Fashion Place in an hour?"

"See you there," he said.

Fashion Place Mall is where we used to meet when we didn't want to run into anyone. There's a little coffee shop at the north end. I got there early and watched the mall denizens shop. It's kind of frightening. The average weekday afternoon shopper is a young woman in her twenties, pregnant, with three or four small children trailing behind like so many blond ducklings in a row, each a head taller than the next. They all have a slightly glazed look about them. The land of the living dead, Dave calls it.

I'd been there fifteen minutes when Dave joined me. In New York City, where he grew up, you'd make him as a cop right away. He's got that cop habit of unconsciously glancing around every few seconds, like a driver in his rearview mirror. In a Salt Lake City mall he seems a bit out of place.

"Coffee," he said to the waitress, sliding into the booth across from me.

"Cream?"

"Black."

I held out my cup. "I could use a refill."

"You bet," she said, and brought back the pot.

"So, what have you been up to lately?" Dave asked, stirring a little sugar into his cup.

"Nothing exciting. Yourself?"

"Same old shit, different day. I haven't slept since the shootings." He took a sip of coffee. "Anything from Jennifer?"

"Not a word." I changed the subject. "How's Christine doing?"

"About the same."

I resisted the impulse to say, "That's too bad." Dave's wife and I had never gotten along too well.

"So, what's the deal with these black kids?" I asked.

Dave sighed. "You remember Willie Moore?" I nodded. Willie was a pimp, and on parole last I heard.

"Well, about three months ago, Sandy Carter, one of the girls in the park last night, started hanging around with Willie."

"Hooking?"

"No, just hanging out. Willie was trying to turn her out for sure, but I don't think she was going for it. She just liked his flash. And she loved his cash. You remember the car he drove?"

"Yeah. A Camaro. Dark red. Pinstripes, custom leather." I visualized it in my mind. "No, wait, a Firebird, wasn't it?" Dave nodded. "I see. A Firebird. Like in the field. Interesting coincidence."

"And even more interesting was that she filed a complaint against him last month for rape. Says he poked her at a party on the West Side. It's coming up for trial next week."

"And she's going to put him away for a few years."

"You got it. He already threatened her once."

"You thinking she was the target? The black kids just got in the way?"

"That was the general idea. One of the other girls did get hit, remember."

"So what changed your mind?"

"Willie was in jail that night on a DUI. His car was in the impound lot."

16

"Too bad."

"Yeah. Riggs is still hot for the idea. He says Willie could have hired someone."

"Sure."

"What do you think, Jase? Any way at all one of the girls was the target?"

I thought about it, putting myself back in the park. I saw it again, the bodies jerking and falling.

"Not a chance," I said.

Dave nodded. "That's what I was afraid of."

"You looking at peer groups?"

"What else?"

"Come up with anything?"

"Yeah, I came up with something. Bill Daniels was once at a party and some high school kid called him a nigger."

"Well, there you have it." I signaled the waitress for another cup of coffee. "So where does that leave you?"

"Sandy Carter, the girl Willie raped." he said. "Know who her old man is?"

"Should I?"

"Stanley Carter."

"Chico?"

"The same."

"Ah," I said. "Now that *is* interesting." Chico was the president of the Pharaohs Motorcycle Club, our local version of the Hell's Angels.

"Word is," Dave said, "that Chico was going to do Willie over the rape thing only he couldn't find him. So then he decided to off any black he caught hanging around his daughter."

"Could be. It wouldn't be the first time he's snuffed someone. Did you talk to him?"

"Yeah, if you can call it that. He basically just told me to fuck off." Dave took a large swallow of coffee and made a face. "That's where you come in, Jase."

"Oh?"

"You've got a line into the Pharaohs. I don't."

I nodded noncommittally. "You really think Chico's good for it?"

"You're the biker expert. Gut feeling?"

"No. Not bikers."

"Why not?"

"Not biker style."

"What do you mean?"

I thought for a minute. "You remember J.Q.?" I said.

"Vaguely."

"He used to be a Pharaoh. Not a bad guy, actually, just way into bikes. He was the dope guy. Supplied all the crank. He didn't do much of it himself, just sat around all day drinking beer and working on his bike. He wasn't really very bright."

"Some of them are?"

"Sure, some of them. Anyway, about seven years ago, he got involved in a hassle at the clubhouse with a couple of visiting Banditos. He got pissed because Chico wouldn't back him, so he decided to get even by setting him up on a dope deal."

"Oh, real smart."

"I told you he wasn't that bright. So, the deal went down, Chico ended up doing some time, and J.Q. decided to leave town."

"Ah. Some faint glimmerings of intelligence, after all."

"Well, not all that much. He only moved as far as Price—didn't even leave the state. He did change his name, though, and for a while it looked like he might be okay. Then gradually he started hanging around the bars at night, and every time a chopper came through town he'd run down and start talking bikes. He just couldn't give up the life. He hooked up with two outlaw bikers from back East, no club affiliation, no colors. They would come by the bar, pick him up, and take off for some good times. Then one day they dropped by his house, put him in their truck, and took him out for a little ride."

"Okay," Dave said. "Now I remember."

18

"Uh-huh. He was found three days later up in Bell's Canyon. Shot, stabbed, strangled with a cord, and then pulled behind a truck for a couple of miles."

"Yeah," said Dave. "And the word 'snitch' was carved in what was left of his forehead."

"Right. That's your typical biker killing. When bikers do a job, you're talking total overkill. They've got to make it a statement. Chico might have hung those kids from a lamppost on State Street, but he wouldn't pull this type of shit, hiding in the bushes with a rifle."

"Yeah, maybe," said Dave. "Still . . ."

"Okay, okay," I said. "I'll see what I can come up with."

"Good enough. By the way, you know Wilton Parker?"

"Sure." Everybody knew Wilton. He was a prominent black attorney who made a hobby of suing government departments on discrimination cases.

"Well, he doesn't have much faith in our ability to handle this one."

"I'm not sure as I blame him, with Riggs in charge."

"He's offered a reward for the killer. Ten thousand dollars for information leading to the arrest, conviction, etcet."

"Not bad."

"Cops aren't eligible."

"But ex-cops are?"

"Exactly. Might be worth a little of your time."

"Could be," I said.

AFTER DAVE LEFT I HEADED DOWN TO SECond West to see Brenda. She held a straight job at Colson Insurance but spent most of her spare time with the Pharaohs. Sort of a weekend warrior. She was my in to the Pharaohs; anything she didn't know she could find out. Assuming, of course, that she felt like it. Most of her information was on trade; I helped her, she helped me, but sometimes she would come through for reasons of her own.

Colson Insurance takes up the ground floor of one of those new steel and glass buildings that Salt Lake proudly takes as a sign of progress. The fact that half the offices are empty doesn't seem to concern anyone. There was a parking space right in front of the building—that's one thing I'll give Salt Lake; you can always find a place to park.

Actually, Salt Lake's not a bad city. Wide streets, manageable traffic, mostly breathable air. The streets get plowed. The garbage gets picked up. Hospital emergency rooms actually have time to treat you. It takes half an hour to register your car. It's got the mountains. It's got the Utah Symphony, Ballet West, and of course, the Utah Jazz.

It's a bit antiseptic for my taste, though. It has a disturbing sameness to it. On any city street the sea of faces is mostly white, all with the identical bland stamp, a heritage from the early Mormon pioneers with their small gene pool, plural marriages, and large families. There are few panhandlers to harass the solid citizen, but there are also no street musicians or sidewalk vendors. Such disruptions of the public order are simply not allowed in the Land of Zion.

And of course, hovering above all, as subtle and omnipresent as the very air you breathe, is the Mormon church. And despite what they want to believe, the Land of Zion isn't all milk and honey. There's a darker side to the city. Ted Bundy once stalked his victims on Salt Lake's pleasant streets, and as every cop knows, rape and murder are common occurrences here. Still, there are worse places to live.

Musing on that, I pushed through the glass doors with COLSON INSURANCE lettered on them and walked into the front office. It was empty of people, and bare except for a row of attached chrome chairs, a few leased plants, and some marginally abstract prints on the walls. Early dentist office decor.

Brenda was sitting alone at a computer terminal next to a telephone console, white blouse and blue skirt half hidden by the large front counter. She heard the door open, but didn't look up.

"I'll be with you in just a moment," she said, frowning at the computer screen.

A few strands of wispy red hair had escaped from her neat bun. I marveled at how anyone as fond of drugs and bikers as she was could appear so virginal and innocent. Not for the first time, I wondered what her co-workers, mostly Mormons, would do if they had any idea what Brenda was really like. Pass out cold, most likely. Brenda was careful, though; she kept her life carefully compart-mentalized.

"Can I help you?" she said, giving the keyboard a final swipe and swiveling her chair around.

"Maybe," I said.

Brenda stared at me, then looked over her shoulder to see if anyone else was in the office.

"Jesus Christ," she said. "Talk about a ghost from the past. This is too weird. I was just thinking about you the other day."

"You must be psychic."

"No really, I was. Hey, you're not still a cop or anything, are you?"

"Nope."

"Well, that's something, anyway. Geez, it's been what, a year?"

"Close to."

"I guess. So what you been doing all this time?"

"Oh, stuff. This and that. I thought I'd drop by and say hello. Just for old times' sake."

"Sure, Jase. And I'm Marie Osmond."

"Brenda, I'm hurt. What are old friends for?"

"In your case, because you want something, I bet. You

sure you're not still a cop?" She fished a cigarette out of her purse and looked over her shoulder. "I'm not supposed to smoke at work. If the boss walks in, you grab it, okay?" She lit up and leaned across the counter. "So?"

"You hear about those two black kids who were shot over in Liberty Park?" I asked.

"Geez, yeah," she said, serious. "That was awful, you know? Sick, like."

"You know that one of the girls who was with them is Chico's daughter?"

"Sandy? Sure. Everybody knows that."

"You know the cops think Chico set the whole thing up?"

"What, the kids getting shot?"

"Yeah."

"You're putting me on."

"Nope. True story. That's what I heard."

"Chico?" She laughed. "No way."

"Why not? I know Chico pretty well, well enough to know he doesn't care much for blacks. Then there's that whole thing with Willie Moore, and then Sandy's hanging around with these other black kids, and then they're dead. Makes you think."

"Makes *you* think, maybe." She grinned. "So you know about Willie, huh?"

"Some."

"Well, you don't know Chico as well as you think. I was at the clubhouse the night Sandy told him about that. She was crying and cursing, talking about how Willie had raped her and everything. She wanted Chico to take care of Willie, fuck him up or kill him or something. You know what Chico said?"

"What?"

Brenda straightened up in her chair and lowered the pitch of her voice, giving a pretty fair imitation of Chico's drawl. "'Sandy, you're sixteen years old now. Old enough to know who's who and what's what, to judge a person's worth, black or white. You chose to hang around with that dirtbag nigger. I told you not to. You told me you'd do what you damned well pleased. Hope you learned something from it.'"

"That was it?"

"That was it. He could care less."

"That's a little hard to swallow," I said.

"Hey, I'm sorry, that's what he said."

"Why didn't he just tell the cops that?"

"Chico? Chico's not gonna tell a cop squat. You know that."

"Hmm," I said.

"Cops. Geez, they can be stupid."

A door in the back of the office opened and a tall office type looked in. I took the cigarette out of Brenda's hand and took a drag. I almost choked. It was menthol.

"Brenda honey," he said, "don't forget I need those claims on Miller by tomorrow morning."

She smiled and nodded at him. "Okay," she said. He pulled his head back and closed the door.

"Christ, how can you smoke those things?" I asked.

"It's to cut down. You have to really want a cigarette to smoke one."

That was certainly true. I handed it back to her and lit one of my own to get the taste out of my mouth.

"Did you know those two black kids?" I asked.

Brenda shook her head. "Just friends of Sandy's, that's all I know."

"How about the other girls?"

"I don't really know them either. Sandy brought them by the clubhouse a couple of times." She took a drag on her cigarette. "One of them, Debbie, was okay. But that other girl—" Brenda shook her head. "You talk about a piece of work."

"You know her name?"

"Monique, I think, something like that. Sandy brought them over to the clubhouse a couple of months ago, and this Monique was real calm for a while, real quiet. Sat around kind of wide-eyed, you know? Then she gets up and walks over to Badger Willie, sweet as can be, and asks him if he ever killed anyone."

"Not cool." A logical question considering the Badger, but definitely not cool. Badger Willie was one of the more psycho club members. I'd never met him, but I'd heard a lot.

"No shit. Badger just looks at her for about a minute, and she stands there looking back at him, and finally she starts to walk away. As soon as she turns away, Badger grabs her, lifts her right up off her feet, and pins her against the wall. Geez, I thought he was going to kill her right there."

"Did he?"

"Nah. I guess he was in a good mood that day. He just looks at her real serious and tells her how he once slit the throat of a cute little girl that looked just like her because she asked too many questions. You know, just fucking with her. You know what she said? She asked him how it felt to cut someone's throat. Swear to God, I think it made her hot."

"What did Badger say?" I asked, laughing.

"He said it was the biggest fucking thrill of his life. You think that threw her? Get this, she looks at him and wiggles her ass and says, 'Did you fuck her afterwards?'"

"Sounds to me like the Badger finally met the girl of his dreams."

"She was way out there, Jase. I mean out there." Brenda frowned. "I think she had something going with one of those colored kids, too, that's what Sandy said."

"Which one?"

"I don't know, one of them."

"Any idea where she is now?"

"Nope."

"Think Sandy might know?"

"Sandy's gone. Chico's already shipped her off to her mom in Texas."

"That's convenient."

Brenda shrugged. "Hey," she said. "I hear there's some money for information about all this. You gonna remember where you got it?"

"Trust me," I said.

3

Brenda's line on Chico's attitude sounded like the truth, unfortunately. It looked like the biker angle wasn't going to fly. I headed home, thinking things over.

Home was a cabin in Little Cottonwood Canyon up in Alta that I was house-sitting for the summer. Little Cottonwood is south and east of Salt Lake City, about forty-five minutes away. When the valley is sizzling, the canyon is cool. It's a great place to spend a summer.

I stopped at the Alta town post office. It occupies a square wooden frame structure that doubles as the volunteer fire department building. Downstairs is the bay for the fire trucks. Upstairs is the library, open one afternoon a week, which doubles as a polling place for elections. Small towns are like that. Everything doubles as something else.

I waved a greeting at Ross, one of the town cops. Alta has a three-man department; it's not exactly a metropolis. Elaine, the postmistress, town clerk, and whatever, handed me my mail. The top letter was torn and frayed on one corner.

"Pot-guts," she explained, using the local name for

ground squirrels. "Yesterday they got in my bureau and chewed up a winter sweater. Don't you have a cat I could borrow?"

"If I could only find him," I said over my shoulder as I left.

The mail was mostly the usual bunch of junk, but the third piece down made me stop. I stood staring at the letter in my hand. It was postmarked Portland, Ore., addressed in a neat, feminine handwriting. The name on the return address read *Jennifer Lassen.*

Jennifer. The lady who changed it all. Jennifer, the love of my life, or so I had thought. But some very bad things had happened to us. I was a homicide cop at the time and I thought I knew what I was doing. By the time it was over, people had died, Jennifer had left, and I wasn't a cop anymore. In fact, I was lucky not to be wearing a number at Point of the Mountain, rubbing shoulders with the very individuals I had put there over the years. Very lucky.

I stuck the letter in my back pocket and headed up to the cabin. On the way I tried not to think about it. I didn't succeed.

The cabin was fifteen minutes from the town office over a dirt road, half hidden in a stand of Engelmann spruce, right where the road curves for the second time. The bottom half has two small bedrooms and a bathroom and the top is one large room with a kitchen built into the back wall. A giant stone fireplace constructed by hand with rocks from the side of the mountain dominates the room. A wooden porch that looks down the canyon hangs over a steep drop. The nearest house is fifty yards away, used only on weekends. My mountain home was a perfect place to invite a young lady for a romantic evening, though ever since Jennifer I hadn't made much effort along those lines.

At the cabin I tossed the letter on the mantelpiece, unopened. I made some coffee, a new blend of Celebes and Kona beans I was trying. When it was ready, I poured a cup, picked up the letter, went outside on the porch, sat down on the bench by the railing, and opened it.

I was disappointed. The letter was all of two lines long. I read them slowly. "Jason. If you still want to see me, I'd like to see you. Call me if you do. Jennifer." There was a phone number with a Portland area code at the bottom.

I didn't know what to feel. Some anger. I hadn't heard from Jennifer since she left last summer. I had got on with my life. Some relief. Even some hope, maybe. Then, sudden desire, so physically strong it made me get up from the bench and walk back inside.

I needed some time to think about it. A lot of time. I put a record on the turntable, Joe Pass and Zoot Sims, just guitar and saxophone. One of the things that came with the cabin was a huge pair of Klipsch speakers, each one the size of a small refrigerator. They were fifteen years old and still outperformed most things on the market. It was going to be hard to leave them when I had to move back down to the valley.

After a while I went back outside and looked around for Stony, the black and white patchwork cat who had moved in with me about five years ago. Which was about five years longer than my thing with Jennifer had lasted. Now he was gone, too. I was turning out to be a hell of a detective. I was trying to find a missing girl and I couldn't even find a missing cat.

When I moved up the canyon I brought Stony with me. I thought he would be in kitty heaven, with an endless supply of pot-guts and all those woods to roam. He hated it. Cats get more attached to places than to people. They stake out their territory and don't like to start over. He had been moping around all summer and I hadn't seen him for days now. I called him a couple of times and then gave up. If he was all right, he'd turn up sooner or later. If he wasn't, there wasn't much I could do about it. Kind of the way the cops felt about Monica.

28

I set up my little hibachi grill on the porch and waited for the charcoal to be ready. As soon as the coals were hot I threw on a steak from the fridge. I thought about a salad but decided it was too much trouble. When I finished I poured another cup of coffee, lit up a Pall Mall, and watched the sun go down behind Superior Mountain. Purple and gold; shadow and light. A Clark's nutcracker flew down onto the railing and eyed me, unafraid. Those are tough birds. Even Stony knew better than to mess with them. It sidled along the rail, regarding the remainder of the steak sitting on my plate. I was saving it in case Stony came home, but I threw the bird a small piece anyway. He hopped down, speared it with his long beak, and flew back up to a nearby spruce. A Steller's jay immediately challenged him for it, and they went at it, squawking and flapping. Try to do someone a favor.

I cleaned up, got out my notebook, and tried to make a list of what I knew about the jogger murders. It wasn't much, and thoughts of Jennifer kept interrupting. After a while I gave up and headed down the mountain to Jimmy's.

Jimmy's is the closest thing Salt Lake has to a neighborhood bar, although there's not much of a neighborhood around it and it's not really a bar. There aren't any real bars in Salt Lake, because you can't buy a drink in any of them. Beer only, and 3.2 beer at that. If you want a drink, you have to buy a minibottle from a state package agency and bring it with you. The bar provides the set up. If you're from out of state, good luck in finding a package store. They're not allowed to advertise. And try finding a listing in the phone book. (It's in the government listings, under Utah State Government, Alcoholic Beverage Control Department.)

I used to say it could be worse, and now it is. The legislature passed two-hundred-and-seventy-pages worth of new laws to control the sale of alcohol, and the bottom line is that places like Jimmy's will be hard-pressed to stay in business as soon as the laws go into effect. Another advantage to living in Happy Valley.

Still, Jimmy's has a scarred oak bar that curves around a corner and some shabby booths with real leather on the seats instead of vinyl. A faded Coors sign in flaking gold paint adorns the front window. Jimmy himself was usually behind the bar. He didn't make enough on the place to hire much help. People came from all over the valley to meet there or listen to the jam sessions in the back room, but not enough of them. Jimmy's is a jazz bar, and the jazz scene in Salt Lake City is pretty small.

A few of the regulars waved at me when I walked in. Ray Prothro. Dave Ritchie. Johnny Starks and his wife, Holly, signaled me to join them, but I wanted a booth closer to the music. Most of the people who hung around at Jimmy's knew I used to be a cop, but they didn't care. I had sat in with the musicians there a couple of times on amateur night, and credentials as a player meant all was forgiven. Jimmy's is one of the few places in the city where I feel at home.

Kevin Stewart was in the middle of a number, comping behind Reggie Dalton on alto. Kevin looked up and nodded at me. He was playing his vintage Gibson, a blond ES-330 he'd packed with cotton to mute and mellow the tone. A great guitar. Reggie was in the middle of a solo and I had to listen a few minutes to figure out what tune they were playing. I finally settled on "Oleo," but it was just a guess until they came back in on the head at the end. There wasn't any drummer, and the bass player was a young kid with glasses and short hair who looked like a computer nerd. He could play, though. He had that vague, slightly spaced look that seems to be a trademark of good bass players. Maybe it's because they have to pay such close attention to the music. The bass player never gets to lay out. In a sense they're always soloing, except they also have to fit their solos around what everyone else is playing.

30

They finished up and started right in on "Joy Spring," a classic Clifford Brown tune. Jimmy's was about half full, but it would be busier later. I got a draft from Jimmy and slipped into the booth closest to the players. The booths at Jimmy's are small, a little cramped for my six feet, and I leaned across the table. It was sticky with old beer. I borrowed a towel from the bar and cleaned it off, razzing Jimmy a little about it.

Kevin took an extended solo, eyes gleaming through rimless glasses, bald head reflecting light, round face beaming through his bushy beard. I could hear him humming along as he played, his voice alternating as usual between melodic grunts and a tuneless buzzing. He ended in unison with Reggie, both coming to a dead stop together with a flourish. Kevin and Reggie took a break, came over to the booth, and sat down across from me. The bass player stayed on the floor and was joined by another guitarist and a couple of horn players.

Reggie was wearing his usual outfit, a suit coat and loosened tie over blue Levi's. I'd seen him at work and he wore the same thing there. Reggie worked for IBM and dressed any way he liked. He was the only black in management that IBM had in Utah and he pretty much did what he wanted. They were terrified he'd sue the shit out of them if they said anything.

"So what do you think?" said Kevin, motioning at the bass player.

"He's good. The guitar player sucked, though."

"Oh, come on," Reggie drawled. "He's not bad for a white boy."

"No rhythm."

"I was adopted," Kevin said. "I used to be black."

"So did I," Reggie said.

"You still are."

"I am? Well, shit. Don't tell anyone, you hear? I'll lose my job."

"I thought you people didn't have jobs," I said.

"What can I say? I screwed up."

They both got a couple of Mooseheads from Jimmy and we listened to the new players. The guitar player was a kid named Nathan, maybe twenty-one, not nearly the player Kevin was, but a lot better than I'll ever be. They started right out with "Giant Steps," trying to show off.

"These young guys scare me," Kevin said, indicating the kid with the guitar.

"He's not in your league and you know it," I told him.

"Not yet, maybe. You should have heard me when I was his age. I was pitiful."

"You're still pitiful," Reggie said.

Kevin ignored the crack and wandered off to talk with someone at another table. Reggie stayed, swirling his beer around in his glass and staring into it. Every once in a while he would take a sip.

"Hey, Jase," he said after a while. "You used to be a cop, right?" I nodded. "I need some advice."

"You in trouble?"

"Not me. Michael. My sister's boy."

"How old is he?"

"Sixteen. Going on thirty."

"Dope?"

"Now look at that," Reggie said. "I say the kid's in trouble, you see black musician, and the first thing you think of is dope."

"Wrong. I hear 'sixteen' and the first thing I think of is dope. Am I wrong?"

Reggie laughed. "As a matter of fact, you're right. But that's not really what I'm worried about."

"So what is?"

"You hear about those two kids that were killed in Liberty Park?"

I nodded. "Who hasn't?" I didn't tell him I'd seen the whole thing.

"Well, one of those kids, Isaac, was Michael's best friend."

"That's too bad."

"Yeah, well, here's the thing. He says Isaac was mixed up with a girl who was in some sort of cult thing, the Church of the Triangle, or some shit like that. The main man is some dude with a weird name. Isaac told Michael about half of the stuff they do, and the half I hear, I don't like."

"Such as?"

"Rituals. Power trips. Weird stuff, sacrificing dogs and cats, shit like that."

"He tell the cops that?"

"Shit, he won't hardly talk to me. He's not going to talk to cops."

"Think he'd talk to me?"

Reggie swallowed some beer. "I doubt it. If he's not gonna talk to the cops he's not gonna turn around and talk to some white dude."

"But I'm not just some white dude. I'm one of your friends."

"Trust me, Jase. You're some white dude."

"Sorry," I said.

"Hey, it's okay. You can't help it. Seriously, Jase, do you think this shit could have anything to do with it? I mean, they kill animals, so why not people?"

"Well," I said, "anything's possible, I guess." I leaned back in the booth. "You wouldn't happen to know that girl's name, would you?"

Reggie shook his head. "So what do you think, should I go to the cops with this?"

"Tell you what," I said. "Let me check this out a little. If there's anything to it, I'll let the homicide guys know."

"Sounds good," Reggie said, relaxing. "I don't really like talking to cops anyway."

Johnny and Holly Starks joined us at the table, and after a while Reggie and Kevin got back up to play. I stayed at Jimmy's for a couple of hours listening, and then drove back up the canyon. Stony still wasn't around. The mountain air was chilly, but I put on a sweatshirt and sat out on the porch anyway, watching the moon rise over Devil's Castle. I listened to the quiet. A slight breeze bent the tops of the trees, bringing the tang of spruce and fir into my lungs. Right before I went inside, a great horned owl, dead silent, enormous in the pale light, floated by no more than twenty feet over my head. I hadn't seen him until he was right on top of me. It was almost supernatural, like a messenger of God. The message, as always, was obscure.

I thought about Jennifer for a while. Maybe I should call her. Maybe not. When I finally went to bed, I dreamed, but not about her.

4

Next day I met Dave at St. Mark's Hospital, where he was going to talk to Debbie Shaw, the girl in the park who was hit. I filled him in on the biker angle. He agreed it didn't look promising. I also mentioned what Reggie had told me about Isaac and a possible cult involvement. He wasn't overly impressed.

"Occult bullshit," was his reaction. "We've got real stuff to look at. You want to sit in while I talk to Debbie?"

"Volter's not going to like it."

"Fuck Volter," he said, and started for the elevator.

We ran into Debbie's doctor right outside her room, a young guy with a neat beard and gold-rimmed glasses and fatigue in his eyes. He stopped us, very fussy, then relaxed when Dave identified himself.

"How's she doing?" Dave asked.

He hunched up his shoulders and sort of bobbed from side to side. "All right, I guess. Her leg's not too bad, considering. She's still pretty upset, though. Talks a lot about people coming to get her. Pretty paranoid."

"Maybe she's got reason," I said. "That is a gunshot wound, after all."

"Hmm, yes, I see what you mean. But she's also . . . well, go talk to her, you'll see what I mean."

"She doped up?"

"I just gave her a shot of Demerol, but she's still pretty lucid. She can talk okay."

"Thanks," Dave said, and pushed open the door.

There were two beds inside the room. The one closest to the window held a middle-aged lady with an IV in her arm, asleep or, for all I knew, in a coma. Debbie lay in the bed nearest the door, and looked up at us as we came in. There was curiosity in her eyes, but no fear. That meant if she was afraid of anyone it was someone she knew. She was still wary, though, more like a suspect than a victim.

She looked very young lying there in the hospital bed. Her pale face and the long hair spilling down over the bed-sheet reminded me of a Pre-Raphaelite painting, the one of the girl floating down a stream, covered in flowers. An interesting face, ethereal almost, the kind you see sometimes in religious fanatics. And in total psychotics. There was a chair next to the bed and another against the wall. I pulled the one near the wall a little closer.

"Well, Debbie," Dave said, fatherly, sitting down in the chair closest to the bed, "so how are you feeling?"

She answered in a thin, shivery voice. "Okay, I guess."

"You feel well enough to talk to us about what happened?"

She looked at Dave for a moment, then asked, "Who are you?"

"Detective Warren. I'm from the police department."

Debbie started to say something but the sound of the door opening behind us interrupted. A young man walked in. He looked like an apprentice mortician, with a white blotchy face and dark lifeless hair lying flat against his head. Debbie didn't seem surprised to see him. He didn't seem too surprised to see us with her, either.

"Good afternoon," he said. "The doctor told me there were a couple of police detectives with Debbie. A terrible thing, wasn't it?"

"Detective Warren," Dave said, getting to his feet. He didn't introduce me.

"Pleased to meet you," said the man. His speech had the peculiar stilted quality of someone who knew all the proper phrases of polite conversation but hadn't had the opportunity to use them much. We waited expectantly until he continued.

"Oh, of course. Sorry. My name is Levi Shaw. Debbie's brother."

"Half brother," Debbie said from the bed.

"Technically, yes, half brother," he agreed, turning to Debbie. "Are you ready to come home?"

Debbie didn't say anything, just sort of scrunched up in the bed. I was getting some funny vibes from both of them. It didn't seem like the usual runaway and family situation. I walked over and stood next to him. Up close, I could smell the odor of soap and new clothes.

"Could I talk to you a minute in private?" I said, taking his elbow and guiding him back out through the door. He couldn't very well resist without struggling with me, so he came along. When I got him back out in the corridor I looked at him long enough to make him self-conscious. He looked back and shifted his weight from one foot to the other. I waited until he was just about to speak, then interrupted.

"Debbie doesn't seem to want go home very much," I said. "What's the problem?"

"Oh, nothing really," he said.

"Discipline? Boys? Drugs?"

"No, nothing like that. She's just . . . well, Debbie is having a little trouble adjusting."

"Adjusting how?"

"Well, we have a sort of extended household."

"Oh. A religious household, perhaps?"

"Precisely."

Polygamy isn't rampant in the State of Utah anymore, but it still isn't all that uncommon, either. It presents a problem for law enforcement, given certain political realities. Enforcing the statutes against it would open up a large can of worms that no one wants to deal with. Mostly the whole thing is quietly ignored.

Most of the polygamous groups are honest and sincere, even a bit straitlaced, but some of them are just flat-out crazy. The Laffertys. The Le Barons. The whole Singer household. A lot of death hangs around those groups. I looked at him with renewed interest and he blushed, understanding what was going through my mind.

"We're not like that," he said. "Not at all. We're just worried about Debbie. This isn't the first time she's run away, and she hasn't always been found with the most savory of characters."

I liked that—*the most savory of characters.*

"That may be," I said, "but right now she's still recovering. I don't think she's ready to go anywhere quite yet."

"I think she'd do better if she were home."

"That's a matter for the doctors to decide, don't you think?"

There wasn't much he could say. He could make a fuss and pull her out, but the polygamous groups that survived did so by learning to keep a low profile and avoiding confrontations with bureaucracy. He blathered on for a while and finally said, "Well, whatever they think is best. We're just worried about Debbie."

Or what she might say, I thought.

I got the address of the family home, one of those big farmhouses out in Riverton, and wrote it on a scrap of paper. Your true professional is never without a scrap of paper. I told him someone would be in touch and waited until he got back on the elevator.

38

Back in the room Dave was still talking to Debbie, or at least trying to, but she had turned her head toward the wall and wasn't saying anything. She turned her head back toward me when she saw I was alone.

"Where's Levi?" she asked.

"Gone home."

"Is he coming back?"

"When you feel better, maybe. Why did you run away, anyhow? Do they treat you so bad?"

She made a face. "Oh, they're all right. But it's such a bore. They want you to work all the time. No movies. No records. No going out. They won't even let me go to school now. Thayne says I don't need to anymore."

"Thayne? Who's Thayne?"

"He's just Thayne, that's who. You know, like God is just God?" She said it half sarcastically, half seriously.

"Are you one of his wives?" I asked. Dave didn't change his expression, but I knew he was caught by surprise.

She giggled. "No, I'm one of his daughters. But he likes me, you know?" She was talking a little slower now, slurring her words a little, and I realized the Demerol was beginning to take hold. "Thayne's old. As old as time. Old. But he's part of the Blood." She giggled again. "I'm part of the Blood, too. We all are."

She lowered her already soft voice to a whisper. "You want to know a secret? About blood? I keep it in my room." She caught the glance Dave threw me. "No, really. I have a jar, a mason jar. I keep it in the closet, on the top shelf. Every night I take a little blood from my arm and put it in the jar. Just a little. But it's almost full now. Then, when they lock me in my room, I can play." She yawned. "They don't like me when I do that." She yawned a little wider. "I don't care what they like. I do what I want." She murmured something I couldn't quite catch.

"What's that, Debbie?" I asked, leaning closer.

"'Do What Thou Wilt,'" she murmured.

Straight from Aleister Crowley. I don't know a lot about

occult groups, but those words are famous, a red flag. Maybe there was something to this cult idea.

"Is that what Thayne says?" I asked quietly.

She shook her head, amused. "Oh, no," she said. "Not Thayne."

"Who, then?"

Debbie turned away, not answering. Dave started to say something but I held up my hand. I let Debbie lie there silently until she started drifting out, then leaned down close to her.

"Is Monica okay?" I asked.

"Don' know," she mumbled.

"Where is she?"

She half opened her eyes. "Monica? I don' know. Maybe with Roger."

"Roger?" I prompted.

"Roger. Roger Dodger."

"Who?"

"Roger Dodger Dodger." Her voice trailed off again and she closed her eyes. I couldn't tell if she had really drifted out or if she was faking it.

"We'll come back later, Debbie," Dave said.

She smiled dreamily. "They love me," she said.

We couldn't get anything more out of her.

"SPOOKY," SAID DAVE AS WE LEFT THE HOSpital. "Definitely spooky. So who's this Monica?"

"Good question. Remember I told you the kid Isaac had some girlfriend into weird shit? That's her."

"Yeah, but who is she?"

"A girl I've been looking for, a runaway. She was there at the park." I remembered Marie Gasteau sniffing, with her orange hair. "Living with some nigger" was the way she had put it.

"You think she's involved in some way?"

"Hard to say."

"Jesus Christ. Bikers. Occult groups. Polygamists. What next?" He thought for a moment. "What did Debbie's brother have to say for himself?"

"Nothing much. They live out in Riverton. She can't fit into the polygamous scene there."

"You think it's connected?"

"Hard to say," I said again, pausing as we reached his car. "Listen, how about running a check on Roger Dodger?"

"Roger Dodger? You really want me to run, 'Roger Dodger?'"

"Why not? It could be his real name."

Dave looked skeptical, but he leaned inside his car, picked up the mike from the dashboard, and switched over to the service channel.

"Dispatch, five-two-five," he said into the mike. "Would you run a records check for me?"

"Ten-four. What is the name?"

"Last Name Dodger: Delta, Oscar, Delta, Golf, Echo, Romeo. First name, Roger. I don't have a DOB."

There was a slight pause. "Ten-four."

I thought I could detect a hint of amusement in the dispatcher's tone, but I wasn't sure. After about thirty seconds she came back, and this time there was no doubt.

"Checking, R-R-Rogerdodger," she said, rolling her "r"s, trying to be cute. "No record found."

"Ten-four," Dave answered.

"R-R-Roger," she said, and I could hear snickering in the background.

Dave hung up the mike on the dashboard. "Satisfied?" he said.

I WASN'T SATISFIED. THE WHOLE OCCULT business was probably flaky, but this Monica kept coming up whenever I talked to anyone. Monica and weird shit. They seemed to go together. Find Melvin, I thought. When you're talking weird shit, the guy you want to talk to is Melvin. Melvin could be difficult, though.

His usual hangout was Washington Square Park, a small patch of green barely a hundred yards square surrounding the Salt Lake City-County Building. It's the only place to really stretch out and rest in the downtown area, so it acts as a magnet to street people. During the summer evenings, groups stand or sit on the grass, staring at the passing world of respectable citizens with sullen and hostile eyes. Every male carries a sheath knife on his belt, partly for protection, but more as a badge of identification. The knife proudly proclaims his status as an outcast of society.

It was close to five when I drove by. The usual crowd had assembled and the sound of laughter mixed with occasional shouts and curses was clearly audible across the street. Straight citizens on their way home from work peered in curiously, eager for a glimpse into an alien world. They did not, I noted, actually enter the park.

I parked across the street and walked into the square, strolling along the curved path that leads from one corner to the other, not hurrying. I recognized a few of the park regulars who were gathered on the benches and tables and got a few dark looks in return. A couple of them drifted farther back in the shadows under the trees, but most of them paid me no mind. The only people they really worried about were the narcs.

Melvin was sitting on a bench table in the back of the park, wearing a long-sleeved plaid shirt and a cheesy cowboy hat. I couldn't ever remember how old Melvin was, although I could have looked it up on his rap sheet. Somewhere between thirty and fifty, with one of those pinched western faces that makes it hard to judge a person's age.

I could see him watching me as he talked to one of his buddies on the bench, so I turned away and walked out of the park. As soon as I was out, I went down a block and around the corner out of sight. I leaned up against the Judge Building and waited, lighting a cigarette. Five minutes later, Melvin came tripping along and I pushed myself away from the building and fell into step with him.

"Coulter," he greeted me. "Hey, man, what's shakin'? I knew you'd want to see me. I knew it. It's those kids, right? Those two colored kids?" He didn't wait for me to answer. "Forget it. You guys are never going to solve that one. They don't want you to."

"Who is 'they,' Melvin?" I asked, obligingly.

"Man, you know. The FBI."

Melvin was an alcoholic, a petty thief, and always in some sort of trouble. Also, he was crazy. He had that most classic of all delusions: the FBI was out to get him because he "knew too much." His delusion was very specific: it was the FBI, and didn't extend to other cops. In fact, he liked cops. Melvin had fed me a lot of information over the years.

What really pushed him over the edge, though, was what happened one particular summer's day. Melvin was standing outside the blood bank, minding his business, looking for someone or something to rip off. Like all good street people, he kept constant watch on the activity around him, glancing up and down the street every few seconds, just keeping an eye on things. Across the street from him, a half block away, stood a man with neatly trimmed hair and a dark business suit. This in itself was enough to draw Melvin's attention, but he also noticed that the man was a Tongan. Very strange. Melvin was crazy, but he was also street smart, very quick to pick up on anything out of place. And this guy didn't fit.

Even worse, as far as Melvin was concerned, was that the Tongan seemed to be paying a little too much attention to that particular corner. He would look quickly at Melvin, then look away, then look down at something in this hand, and then look back at Melvin again.

This sort of behavior would be enough to make anyone nervous, let alone a petty thief with paranoid delusions. Melvin got more and more uptight, until finally he decided to split and took off down the block. The Tongan crossed the street, and began to follow him.

What Melvin didn't know was that the Tongan was actually an FBI agent. In his hand was a photo of a man who had robbed a downtown bank the day before. The bank's hidden camera got his picture, which unfortunately bore a distinct resemblance to Melvin. The agent caught up with Melvin a block away and uttered those fateful words, the words Melvin had been fearing and dreading most of his life.

"FBI," he said, displaying his badge. "Hold it right there."

Melvin uttered a strangled shriek, jumped back, and pulled out the hunting knife he always wore on his belt. His worst fears had been realized, but they weren't going to take him without a fight.

Of course, all the agent knew was that he had stopped a bank robbery suspect and the man had gone berserk and pulled out a large knife, with obviously homicidal intentions. Like most FBI agents, he had little practical experience in dealing with street confrontations, but he drew on all his professional expertise and common sense. He grabbed his gun and shot Melvin in the stomach. Melvin fell to the ground, and the agent, who had never before fired his gun, stood there for a moment, stupefied. It was the last thing he had expected to happen. But he was a trained agent, and he reacted the way an FBI agent is trained—he immediately walked across the street and called his supervisor.

I was on stakeout that day two blocks away, and when Dispatch broadcast a "Man down" call, I was first on the scene. I found Melvin lying on the sidewalk.

"Oh, shit," I said. "Melvin, can you talk? It's me, Jason." Melvin looked up at me and grunted.

"Okay, take it easy," I said. "You're going to be all right. The paramedics are on their way." Melvin grunted again. I thought maybe he wasn't going to be all right. He was bleeding a lot, and his eyes were starting to glaze over. I leaned down and put my face next to his.

"Melvin," I asked urgently, "who shot you?"

He lifted up his head and made a supreme effort. "The FBI," he croaked. "They got me."

I felt like grabbing him by the throat and shaking him. Here he was on his way out, and he still couldn't shake his delusion long enough to tell me who did it.

"Melvin," I pleaded, as gently as I could. "Come on now, man. Forget the FBI stuff. You've got to tell me. Who shot you?"

He looked at me and there were tears in his eyes, whether from pain or frustration I couldn't tell.

"It was them, I tell ya," he wheezed, "the FBI. They got me." Then he passed out.

Eventually, of course, the FBI agent returned and explained what had happened. Melvin survived; he was tougher than he looked. From that time on, though, I couldn't get through to him. Any time I suggested he might be a little paranoid about the FBI, he'd pull up his shirt, show me his scar for the fiftieth time, and say, "Okay, Coulter. Explain this, then." He had a point.

Melvin knew a lot, but it was hard keeping him on track. I hadn't expected his FBI paranoia to surface quite so quickly, though.

"Yeah, the FBI," he said again as we walked along Third South. "They did that hit on the colored kids. They set the whole thing up themselves. You get too close to them and zap—that's it. You got to watch your ass, man." He looked around, suddenly worried. "Fuck, they might be on to us right now."

"No way," I reassured him, shooting him a conspiratorial glance. "I took precautions." Melvin nodded knowingly.

I couldn't resist prodding him a little. "What are they doing mixed up in this anyway?"

"Oh, man," he said, giving me a pitying look. I was just a babe in the woods. "It's the whole racist thing."

"The FBI are racists?"

"Well sure, man, but that's not it. PR. That's the deal. They want to make themselves look good, okay? They set it up, see, they set up the hit and then they sit back and wait. You guys try to solve it and fall on your faces. Then what happens?"

I bit. "What?"

"The papers, man. The TV. Everybody says the cops don't want to solve it. The cops don't really care, 'cause these are just colored kids, right?"

I did a double take. Melvin had just neatly paraphrased what I knew was the department's worst fear. I wasn't sure if this said more about Melvin or the department.

"Then they step in," he continued. "The FBI takes over the case. Boom—twenty-four hours later, the case is solved, and they're fucking heroes, and you guys are dogshit."

I'd worked with the FBI. Believe me, it wasn't near as crazy as it sounds.

"Yeah," I said. "Well, there's nothing much I can do about that, I guess. But listen, forget about the FBI for a minute. You ever heard of a group called the Church of the Triangle?"

"Four-Sided Triangle," he corrected. "The Church of the Four-Sided Triangle. Weird dudes."

"How weird? Dangerous weird?"

"Fuckin' A. Sacrifices, man. Ritual goddamn sacrifices, that's what they're into. They rip their fucking hearts out, man, while they're still alive. They do all that shit."

"Really," I said. "You ever actually see any of this?"

"Fuck, no. I don't have to see it. It happens, man. It happens all the time. I mean, those dudes are bad news."

He held up a finger to emphasize the point, and his shirt-sleeve dropped down, revealing a turquoise bracelet. There was a price tag dangling from it. I pointed to it silently. Melvin tore off the tag quickly, embarrassed.

"Forgot to take off the tag when I bought it," he mumbled.

"Uh-huh. Nice bracelet. Anyway, I'm looking for a girl who might be into this Triangle church. Name of Monica. You know her?"

"Monica. Don't think so. I might if I saw her."

I pulled out her photo from my wallet. Melvin studied it. "Sure, I seen her around. Nice-looking chick."

"You seen her lately?"

He shook his head. "I can tell you one thing, man, any chick tight with those dudes, she's history. Fucking history."

"Who runs it?"

"Runs what?"

"That church."

"It don't matter. It's just a front, anyway."

"A front for who?" I asked, as if I didn't know.

"FBI, man, FBI."

I tried to head him off. "Well, yeah, sure," I said. "But who's the front man? They gotta have a front man."

Melvin looked at me out of the corner of his eye. "You really wanna know?"

"Yeah, I do."

"Can't tell you, man."

"You don't know?"

"Fuck, yeah I know. But I can't tell you."

"Why not?"

"'Cause I could get myself in trouble, that's why not. Besides, you'd think I was crazy."

"Melvin," I said. "I *know* you're crazy."

"No, I'm not."

"Sure you are."

"I wasn't crazy about this, was I?" he said, starting to lift his shirt.

"Okay, okay, I take it back. So, who is this guy?"

"What guy?"

"The guy whose name you won't tell me because you're crazy."

"I told you, I ain't crazy."

"Then why won't you tell me who he is?"

Melvin looked at me, opened his mouth, and shook his head in disgust. "Fuck, Coulter, you're the one who's crazy."

"I never said I wasn't." I stopped and took him by the arm. "Come on, Melvin." I took a twenty out of my wallet. He hesitated a second, then took it.

"Yeah. Well, okay, but remember, keep it quiet."

"Quiet as the grave."

"Hey, man, don't say that."

"Sorry, Melvin. So who is this guy?"

"His name's Narada."

"That a first or a last name?"

"Just Narada. That's all I ever heard."

"Mexican?"

"I don't think so. Just a regular guy. I never met him or anything, but I know about him."

"How?"

"I just do. But if you want to find him, I can tell you where to look."

"FBI headquarters, right?"

Melvin ignored my sarcasm. "You got it," he said.

I wasn't going to get anything else useful out of him. I gave it up and walked back to my car. Time to call it a day. At least I had some names. Narada. The Church of the Four-Sided Triangle. On my way up the canyon I gave it some thought. I wasn't buying the bit about ritual sacrifices, but over the years I'd learned there was usually something behind Melvin's stories, no matter how far out. The trick was to figure out what it was. Melvin was a sort of a psychotic Delphic oracle.

I was looking forward to a leisurely session on the porch with my guitar and a couple of gin and tonics, but the minute I walked in the cabin door I was greeted by a piteous meowing. Stony was home. He came running up to me, or rather hopping up to me on three legs, one paw held up off the ground.

"Oh, no," I said. "What have you done now?"

He just looked up at me and whined like a dog. I bent down to take a look. His right paw was swollen to almost triple its normal size. It didn't look infected. It looked like it was either sprained or broken. I sighed and picked him up. If I was lucky I could get to the vet before they closed.

Usually Stony was pretty quiet in the car so I didn't need a cat carrier, but this time he howled all the way down the canyon. First he threw himself over my neck. Then he curled around the floor shift. Then he wedged himself under the brake pedal just as I entered a curve. It was a long drive.

The vet's office was just closing as I got there, but they took him right in. For once there wasn't anything waiting there trying to eat him. The rest of the news wasn't so good. The vet manipulated his paw around gently, which Stony didn't much care for, and then took an X-ray. After a while, he came out with the film in his hand.

"Just how much does this cat mean to you?" he said.

"What do you mean?"

"Well, nothing's broken, but the ligaments in the paw are all torn. It's possible it'll heal on its own, but what he really needs is surgery to correct it, and that can be expensive."

"How expensive?" I asked. When he told me, I looked down at Stony, and said, "How much to just clip off the paw?"

With perfect timing, Stony raised his head and howled. "Just kidding," I reassured him.

"Tell you what," said the vet. "Let it go for a while and see if it mends any. If not, you can decide what to do then. I'd splint it, but you really can't do that with a cat. They tear them off."

"Oh, well," I said, as I gathered Stony up to leave. "There's nothing wrong with a three-legged cat."

As soon I got him back home Stony crawled off into the corner behind one of the big Klipsch speakers and curled up looking miserable. I took out Jennifer's letter and read it again. Then I picked up the phone. Then I put it down. Then I picked it up. After a few more times of doing this I got out my guitar, an old cherry red Gibson ES-335. Not as nice as Kevin's 330, but I liked it. I started working on chord theory.

Chords are fascinating. The relationships start out simple enough, say, a major chord connected to its relative minor. But that minor chord is also related to a different type of chord altogether. And that different chord to still another. Eventually, you see that all chords are related in *some* way. And all scales. Then, getting deep into it, the illuminating flash comes. The interlocking patterns dissolve and you can almost see it all, the grand design, music as totality. And then, on the verge of truly grasping this mystical vision, I lose it. If you don't lose it, you become Mozart. I'd settle for Duke Ellington.

When I finally noticed the time on the clock, it was far

too late to call. Another problem solved. I foraged in the fridge, coming up with Cheddar cheese and crackers for a late snack. By the time I got to bed it was almost four. When the phone rang at ten the next morning I was still dead to the world.

"Yes," I answered, yawning.

"Must be nice," a voice said. "Sleeping in on a weekday."

"Dave?"

"Amazing. You've still got those old detective instincts."

"Spare me," I said.

"Sure. I just thought you might be interested in checking out a certain Roger Dodgson."

I came fully awake. "Shit. Roger Dodger. You ran it on a Soundex file."

"Yeah. Came up with three names. Roger Dodge, bad checks in 1985, a Roger Dojon with a couple of outstanding traffic warrants, and this fellow, Dodgson."

"What's he got?"

"Nothing much. Two 'contributing to the delinquency of a minor' arrests. I looked up the cases. Both involved harboring runaway girls. Also an indecent exposure charge. Seems he was running around Memory Grove one night without any clothes, stoned as a chicken."

"Sounds like he might be our boy," I said.

"Could be. Worth looking at, if you're still interested."

"You got an address?"

"Just came back—226 Second Avenue, apartment two-F. Somebody else is living there, name of Procter. Never heard of Dodgson."

"You find a manager?"

"Yeah. He says the rent hasn't been paid in two months, and he can't remember the last time he saw Dodgson. He finally just cleared out the place and rented it to this guy Procter."

"So what now?"

"You want to look for him, be my guest. I don't have the

time. Riggs has called a task force meeting with the FBI and I'm doing the briefing."

"The FBI's coming in? What jurisdiction?"

"Civil rights. If the two kids were shot because they were black, it's a civil rights deal. And the bureau wants in on this one."

"And you guys are dogshit," I said, quoting Melvin.

"Not this time. Any of those motherfuckers pull any shit and there'll be another homicide to investigate."

"Some of them aren't so bad."

"Yeah, and some of them are. With my luck, I'll end up with a supervisor."

"Well, good luck," I said.

"Thanks a lot. Now on top of everything else, I've got the fucking FBI to babysit."

"I'll call you if I come up with anything on Dodgson."

"You do that," Dave said, and hung up.

I put some coffee beans in the grinder. Stony heard the whirring and came scrambling through the kitchen window on three paws. I could never figure if he got the coffee grinder confused with the electric can opener or if he just thought that since I was up he might get some breakfast.

The paw looked a little better, down to twice normal sized. He still hopped on three legs, but occasionally he would rest it on the ground when he sat. I started the coffee brewing and gave him a half can of tuna on a paper plate. He devoured it so fast he almost choked. Can you say that a cat "wolfs" down his food? He licked the plate across the floor and looked up at me expectantly.

"No way," I said, pouring a cup of coffee and looking critically at his round belly. "You probably sprained your paw jumping out of a tree. Too much weight."

He yawned unconcernedly and strolled out of the kitchen. No doubt he had other sources.

By noon I was knocking on the door of the manager's apartment at 226 Second Avenue. The Avenues is a nice place to live. Many of the houses are older Victorian types, occupied by upscale young professionals. A few are rented by University of Utah students, three or four to a house. But further away from the U, right where the Avenues bleeds into downtown, there are still a few pockets of semi-slum apartments.

Number 226 was a red brick apartment building that would no doubt be condemned in a few years to make room for condos. In the meantime, it was hanging on, crumbling a little around the corners but still fairly solid.

The man who answered the door was flat faced and bald and hadn't shaved yet that morning. I could hear a TV on in the background, something with a studio audience and a shrill host.

"No apartments available," he said before I could speak.

"I'm not looking for an apartment. I'm looking for one of your former tenants, Roger Dodgson. Detective Warren was here earlier about him."

"Oh, yeah," he said. "Dodgson. Like I said, I ain't seen him in a long time. Rented out the place last month to another party."

"What was he like?"

"Dodgson?" He shrugged. "All right, I guess. No trouble."

"He ever have girls up there? Young girls?"

"Hey, mister, you're a cop. They all got girls. Young, old, in between. As long as they don't cause trouble and they pay the rent, I figure what they do is none of my business."

"I'm not saying it is," I said, nodding in agreement. "You cleared out the apartment before you rented it?"

"Yeah, I did. The guy stiffed me on the rent. If he wants his belongings back, he's gotta pay. Not that he had much stuff. A bunch of books, mostly. Some other junk. Some stuff in drawers. The furniture goes with the place."

"What about the bathroom?"

"The bathroom?"

"Anything left there? Toothbrush, razors, stuff like that?"

The manager caught on immediately. "You think something happened to him?"

"Who knows? Did he clean out the bathroom?"

"Nope. There was a bunch of stuff there. I just threw it in a box with the rest of his shit."

"You still got it?"

"In the basement. You want to take a look?"

"If it wouldn't be too much trouble."

"No trouble." He led the way around to the back of the building, took out a ring of keys, and unlocked a door there. "Watch the steps," he said, leading the way down. "The light's out."

We groped our way through the dim light until we reached the wall opposite the stairs, where he reached up and yanked the pull chain of a naked bulb hanging from the ceiling. He shoved some cartons out of the way and pulled out a large box with Hitachi TV printed on the side.

"This is it," he said. "Told you he didn't have too much."

I squatted next to the carton, reached in and took out a book. *Sane Occultism* by Dion Fortune. Right beneath it was *Psychic Self-Defense* by the same author. It looked like I had the right Roger.

"You need me for anything?" the manager asked. I shook my head and he made his way back through the dimness. I turned back to the carton on the floor.

I went through all the papers in the box. I found a few phone numbers scrawled on bits of paper, which I copied down. Nothing else that looked helpful. Receipts for bills. A recipe for Chicken Marsala. There were some lines of poetry scribbled on a yellow legal pad. They looked pretty obscure, mostly about death from what I could gather. A few cassette tapes of classical music, but no tape player. It was probably in the manager's apartment.

I turned my attention to the books. Most of them dealt with the occult, although a copy of John D. MacDonald's, *The Dreadful Lemon Sky* caught my eye. The only other title I recognized was a hardback copy of *The Theory and Practice of Magick* by Aleister Crowley. I opened it and thumbed through it at random. It seemed kind of dull. Near the back of the book an envelope inserted between the pages fell out. Inside the envelope was a packet of photographs. I stood up and examined them under the light bulb. They were pornographic snapshots of a guy and a girl doing various things to each other. The guy had his back to the camera, but the girl was familiar. I pulled out the photo in my wallet to make sure. It was Monica, all right.

The last shot in the series was of Monica alone on a table draped with black cloth, lying on her back. One leg was cocked to the side and there was a come-hither expression on her face. Not the artificial look of a *Penthouse* centerfold. One that really meant it. She had a perfectly proportioned body, smooth skin, thick pubic hair. Sixteen, I remembered, looking at it with interest. I could empathize with her English teacher.

The backs of the photos were numbered one through ten, written in pencil. Six and nine were missing. I slipped the photos in my wallet and checked the envelope carefully. There was something else inside, four little packages of plastic wrap, each containing a tiny bit of what looked like road tar, maybe a third the size of a match head. Each packet had been twisted shut, the ends sealed by melting them with a flame.

Black tar heroin has replaced the old system of powder in balloons, but it's just as potent. Roger must have intended to come back; nobody abandons their dope.

I carefully placed the chips with the photos and went through the rest of the books page by page. There weren't any more photos, but there was a receipt for Zion Self Storage, lot E-5, dated June 1. It was paid up through the end of the year.

The self-storage companies rent space, everything from the size of a gym locker to a shed big enough to hold a car. It looked like maybe Roger had been planning to leave for a while. That's why there was nothing in the apartment. Whatever he owned would be in the shed. Including, hopefully, some indication of where he might be now.

The storage receipt joined the photos, and on the way out, I knocked on the manager's apartment again.

"You find anything?" he asked when he answered the door.

"Just a bunch of books," I said. I took out the photo of Monica, not one from the packet, the one her parents had given me. "You ever see this girl with him?"

He barely looked at the picture. "I told you," he said, "I don't keep track of who comes and goes here." He looked back into the apartment as a roar of laughter issued from the TV.

"Thanks anyway," I said, and let him get back to his show.

Zion Self Storage was on the West Side of the city, in the industrial area near the I-80 underpass at Sixth South. I drove by to take a look at it. Most people never see that side of their city. Railroad tracks, long unused, crisscross the streets. Auto wrecking yards, container factories, processing plants, detached semitruck trailers, salvage yards, and obscure businesses sprawl through the area, separated by vacant lots and abandoned buildings.

A lot of the transients in Salt Lake hang around there, which meant the storage lot would have to be fairly well secured if it wanted to stay in business. Two men were fighting drunkenly as I drove by the Sixth South overpass, but it didn't look like they were doing each other a great deal of harm. Behind them, on the concrete abutment, somebody had spray-painted a message: LEROY. I WONT HURT OR KILL YOU NO MORE—DELMAR. Eight million stories in the naked city.

I located Zion Self Storage between two warehouses,

right across from a building with MIDWEST CASKETS painted in faded red letters too many years old. An eight-foot wire mesh fence topped by three rusted strands of barbed wire surrounded the lot. The lot was filled with rows of sheds, each large enough for a large car or a small roomful of furniture. Each shed had an overhead sliding metal door secured on the bottom by a padlock. Access to the lot was through a gate on rollers, obviously locked at night. A teenage boy with no shirt sat in a small booth in front. I doubted he would be there at night; twenty-four-hour security cost money, and this was a marginal operation. I parked down the street from the place for about an hour, but no one showed up. It obviously didn't get a lot of traffic.

I wanted a look inside Roger's shed, but I couldn't just walk up and ask for the key. And there certainly wasn't enough of anything for Dave to get a warrant. However, I did have one advantage. I wasn't a cop anymore.

I drove back up the canyon, stopping by an Albertson's on the way to pick up some milk and eggs. In front of me in line stood a Hispanic-looking woman with three kids, one in a stroller, one about three hanging on to her hand, and a little baby in a carrier. The two older kids were raising hell, but the baby was quiet. It was wrapped in a blue flannel blanket with a furry white hat over its head. Little baby-sized sunglasses peeked out from under the hat. Cute. It was kind of overdressed for the weather, though. Maybe it was sick.

The blanket slipped a little as she stepped up to pay for her groceries. I got just a glimpse of the child before she pulled the blanket back up. Unless this lady's last name was Hormel, there was something definitely amiss. Enfolded carefully in the blanket lay what must have been a fifteen-pound ham at least. I looked at the checker, obliviously ringing up items on the register. The Hispanic lady crooned tenderly to the ham as she waited patiently, rocking it gently in her arms. She made it through the checkstand without any problem, I paid for my stuff and caught up to her outside.

"A very beautiful child," I said. "And so quiet." She stared at me with a broad impassive face, then grinned. I grinned back.

Back at the cabin, I put the photos in my desk drawer, made some French toast, sat out on the porch until full dark, washed up, set my alarm for two, and tried to get some sleep. Four hours wouldn't be a lot, but it was better than nothing.

I didn't quite make the full four. About one-thirty I sat bolt upright in bed, adrenaline pumping, jolted awake by the most appalling noise. I was actually reaching for the Walther I keep on the bedside table before I realized it was a catfight in the living room. Stony was at it again, screaming and squalling. By the time I was out of bed and upstairs it was over. Stony was standing at the open kitchen window on his three good legs, staring out and giving voice to an occasional wail. He looked worse than usual, with muddy fur and bright red scratches on his nose. The tip of his left ear was torn. It was raining outside and he was a mess. I peered out and saw the shadow of the other cat ghosting through the trees. It looked like the big black tom who lived a few houses down the canyon, Stony's new bête noire.

"I know," I said. "You can beat him with one paw tied behind your back." He glanced at me disdainfully, standing guard by the window. Finally he hopped down off the sill and began cleaning himself.

At least I was up. I put on dark jeans, threw a windbreaker over a dark T-shirt, and checked the burglar bag I keep under the spare tire well in my Honda. Duct tape, gloves, glass cutter, flashlight, small bolt cutter, pry bar, Super Glue. A few other odd things. Nothing exactly illegal, but still not a good collection to explain if you get shaken down by a cop.

The rain was just ending as I climbed in my car. I

breathed deeply. A few low-lying clouds moved up the canyon, suspended between the peaks. As I drove down into the valley the cool mountain air made the wet road steam, obscuring it in spots. Halfway down I almost hit a deer that tried to commit suicide by throwing himself in front of my car, but I swerved in time.

I arrived at Zion Self Storage about three. The streets were empty, deserted in that special way the industrial part of a small city can be late at night. I parked about a block away, by the overpass. A couple of transients looked up from the corner where they were sleeping, stared at me incuriously, and went back to sleep.

I walked down the block to the front gate of the lot. The booth was empty. I edged along to the end of the fence, right where it met the wall of the warehouse building. Between the end of the fence and the building was a small gap, not big enough to squeeze through, just enough to slip my bag inside. I had been planning to snip the barbed wire, but I wouldn't have to. I climbed up the fence, catching the rounded end of the fence post in my left hand. I used my right to balance myself against the corner of the building, got my left foot over the barbed wire and on the top of the fence proper, put my right foot on top of the fence post, and balanced precariously, still holding the corner of the building. I dropped down to the other side, rolling as I hit to save my knees.

I picked up my bag and slid over to the first row of sheds, out of sight of the street. A quick flash of my light showed that the first shed was A-1, so E-5 should be somewhere in the back. I picked my way along until I reached row E, counted five down and bent down to examine the padlock. Then I straightened up, fast.

There was a faint but unmistakable scent of corruption emanating from the shed. A smell faintly sweet, stirring all sorts of unpleasant memories. Before I worked Homicide, I thought that the phrase "the smell of death" was some kind of literary metaphor, and a clichéd one at that. Not so. The smell of death is real; it not only assaults your senses physically, it reaches down and grabs you emotionally on a very primitive level. Once you smell that smell you never forget it, and the hundredth time is as bad as the first.

I leaned back down and examined the lock. Another surprise. There was no lock. So much for security. I checked with my light to make sure I had the right shed. I did. I thought for a minute. Then I slipped on the gloves from my bag and pulled the sliding door halfway up.

The smell rolled out, stronger, but still not overpowering. I ducked in under the door and stood up. Illuminated by the thin beam of my flashlight sat a dusty yellow Volkswagen. It was parked facing in, and the small rear window was so dirty and smeared that it was almost completely opaque. On the driver's side the window was rolled all the way up except for a small crack at the top which had been stuffed with rags. An ordinary green garden hose was attached to the exhaust pipe and snaked up through the crack in the window, where it was sealed and held in place by gray duct tape. The passenger window was also smeared. I used one of my gloves to wipe an area partly clear and shined my flash inside the car. A face stared back at me, a face that looked like it belonged in a particularly gruesome horror movie. Unless I was mistaken, I had found Roger Dodger.

The worst bodies are a week or two old, bloated and rotten, inspiring no emotion except disgust. After two or three months they are unrecognizable, except as something that might perhaps have once been a human being. But this was different. The body had been partially mummified by the lack of oxygen in the sealed car. The skin on the arms had withered and darkened, until it resembled old leather or parchment. One side of the head had dissolved away and the bone and teeth shone through in the familiar skeleton grin. The other half had dried and puckered, so that he was almost recognizable as an individual. If I had known Roger in life, I would have known him now. Wedged into the back seat of the car, sitting upright, one withered arm still draped along the back of the seat, he stared directly at me. It was as if a childhood horror had come to life, a scene from a Stephen King fantasy somehow become real, the very embodiment of mortality. Through the smeared and dirty glass he stared, threatening to rise up suddenly, grasp my hand, and embrace me with secrets of death that I did not wish to know.

For about ten seconds that seemed like ten minutes, I stood and stared at that peculiar apparition. Finally, I pulled myself together. Dead bodies were nothing new, I told myself. Maybe I'd been out of Homicide too long.

There really wasn't anything for it but to call Dave. I ducked back out of the shed, pulled the door closed, climbed back over the fence, walked back to my car, and drove to the 7-Eleven on Ninth West. It took twelve rings before Dave answered.

"Jason here," I said when he picked up the phone.

"Jesus Christ, Jason, do you know what time it is?"

"Yeah, I do. Meet me at Zion Self Storage, Sixth South and Fifth West. Get Dispatch to locate a manager to let us in."

"What are you talking about?"

"Just meet me there," I said.

Dave was more awake now. "What have you got?"

"Come down and take a look. How long will it take you?"

"Half hour. You need a uniform car?"

"Wouldn't hurt," I said.

I got a cup of coffee, drove back down to the lot, and parked right in front. About five minutes later, a black and white pulled up in back of me. It was another rookie I didn't know. In another couple of years I wouldn't know anyone. He looked like a lineman on a Pro football team, with arms the size of my thighs and a neck to match. He was obviously expecting to find me there, but he kept his hand near his gun until I showed him some ID. I thoroughly approved. You just never know, and a careless cop will someday turn into a dead cop.

Dave and the lot manager arrived within a minute of each other. The manager thought there had been a burglary at the lot and was a bit put off when he found all we wanted him to do was check one of the storage sheds.

"Couldn't this have waited until morning?" he grumbled, unlocking the front gate.

"Sorry, it's important," Dave answered. He looked over at me and I nodded.

I led the way to E-5. Dave got right up to the metal door before he caught that telltale whiff. He stopped and looked at me again.

"Oh shit," he said.

He pulled up the sliding door and went inside with the rookie. I remained discreetly outside for the moment with the manager. Dave was back out in a minute and he pulled me aside.

"You touch anything? There's a place on the window rubbed clean."

"That's all," I said.

Dave started the machinery of death moving: call the crime lab, notify the medical examiner's office, call the mortuary, advise the field commander, and so on.

"You calling Volter?" I asked.

Dave shook his head. "Let him sleep."

The field commander, Jim Hobson, showed up. Jim's pushing fifty but he's in better shape than most of the rookies. Jim runs marathons just for fun. He and I had always gotten along. He went in and took a look at the car. When he came out, he stepped over next to me.

"Now, that is really something," he said. "How did you find him?"

"Just playing a hunch."

"Uh-huh." He glanced over at me. "You know that haunted house the Elks set up every year at Halloween, to raise money for crippled kids? We ought to haul the whole thing over intact as one of the exhibits. It would make a fortune."

The crime lab van pulled up and Jerry Archibald climbed out, camera equipment hanging over him like a burro.

"You do get around," he said to me, unslinging his bag. I shrugged noncommittally.

Jerry set up his camera and got to work. Outside shots of the lot, the shed, and the car inside it. Then the inside shots. When he opened the door of the car to get pictures of the interior the stench became overpowering, and the simple fact of a decomposing body dispelled any lingering morbid fantasies I might have had. I looked inside and saw a cassette player on the dashboard with a partially burned candle sitting on top of it.

It wasn't difficult to reconstruct what had happened. Roger had lighted the candle, turned on the cassette player, and sat listening to the tape and watching the candlelight as his life slipped away. When the carbon monoxide from the exhaust reached a certain level, the candle, along with Roger's life, went out. At least that was the way it was supposed to look. I wasn't so sure.

The mortuary guys showed up to take the body to the M.E.'s office. One of them got in the car, and with Dave's help, managed to get the remains out toward a waiting body bag. I observed. This was one part of the job I didn't miss.

I noticed the rookie looking a bit queasy as he watched. Being a rookie, of course he had to show that nothing bothered him, and he nonchalantly stepped forward as they lifted Roger out.

Although the body looked solid, after two or three months Roger was really rather fragile, and as he came out of the car, his head toppled off, rolled over a couple of times, and came to rest against the rookie's shoe. It lay there looking up at him, somehow horribly keeping its personality even when detached from the body. Without a word, the rookie ran out of the garage and could be heard gagging loudly behind his patrol car.

"They don't make 'em like they used to," said Jim. I wasn't sure if he was referring to the rookie or the body.

The back of the garage was cluttered with boxes. We ignored them for the moment, but as soon as Roger was out, Dave and I did a cursory search of the car. I was breathing through my mouth. It didn't help much.

On the floor of the backseat lay an empty syringe. Dave bagged it and set it aside. We checked the glove box, under the mats, under the front seats. A registration in the name of Roger Dodgson and a repair bill were all we came up with. I looked at the tape in the cassette player. Mozart's Requiem, a nice touch. Maybe it really was a suicide.

By the time everything was cleared away it was light. They didn't need me anymore so I took the long drive back up the canyon. When I got home I found that I couldn't get rid of the smell. It seemed to permeate my clothes. I kept sniffing compulsively at my shirt. I put the clothes in the hamper as soon as I got home, but I could still smell it. I couldn't tell for the life of me whether it was real or my imagination. Finally I gave up, took the clothes back out of the hamper, threw them outside behind the cabin, and took a very long, very hot shower.

6

The phone rang at noon, waking me again. It seemed like getting a full eight hours was something no longer part of my life.

"Yes," I said, groping for a cigarette.

"Up and at 'em, Jase," said Dave's voice.

"Gnaggh," I grunted.

"Bright eyed and bushy tailed, I see. Come on, Jase, wake up. I haven't even been to bed yet."

"You get paid," I said, getting my bearings. I put the cigarette in my mouth and lit it. "How soon can we get the autopsy results on Roger?"

"Sometime tomorrow, probably. Right now I'm down at the Federal Building, talking to the feds. They mentioned they'd like to talk to you, too."

"Me? What about?"

"They didn't tell me and I didn't ask. Just relaying the message."

I sighed theatrically. "Okay, whatever. It'll take me about an hour."

"They'll be waiting for you."

"Anything else? You come up with anything interesting on Dodgson?"

"Not yet. Actually, I'm not going to have much time to pursue it for a while."

"Why not? He knew Monica, Monica knew that kid Isaac, and they're both dead. I mean, it's the only real lead you've got, isn't it?"

"Maybe, maybe not. We're checking every known crazy with a thing for blacks first. Riggs has really zeroed in on that. He's not much interested in anything else."

"So Dodgson's just being considered a suicide, no connection?"

"At the moment."

"Well, okay," I said.

THE FEDERAL BUILDING SQUATS HEAVILY on the corner of First South and State, six stories, row after row of narrow vertical window slits. In the courtyard out front there's a modern stone sculpture in a fake Picasso style. Kids with skateboards sit on it and drum their heels on the granite.

The ground floor lobby is small, dominated by an entire wall of mailboxes. A lot of people mistake it for the post office. I took the elevator to the fifth floor. The Salt Lake division of the FBI isn't that large; it only rates one corner of the floor, but they do their best to make it look impressive.

I pushed open the clear glass door with the seal of the United States on it, which leads into their offices. A heavy-set man sporting a tiny mustache and a pinkie ring sat in one corner. He looked curiously at me, trying to figure if I was an agent, an informant, or a suspect. I did the same. He looked like prime snitch material to me.

The receptionist was walled off from the rest of the office behind a pane of bulletproof glass. She spoke to people through a metal grille, like a bank teller in a high-crime area.

"Can I help you?" she said, running a hand through chopped hair.

"My name's Jason Coulter. Somebody here wants to see me."

"Oh, yes. If you'll have a seat, Agent Whitmore will be right with you."

I sat down in one of the leather chairs. Real leather, very nice. No ashtrays. Photographs of scenic Utah hung on one wall. Across from them was a board of the bureau's TEN MOST WANTED. One of the fluorescent lights in the ceiling was out.

After I'd waited a couple of minutes, the door leading to the inner offices opened and a slick type in a sport coat and gray slacks poked his head out. He glanced back and forth at the two of us sitting there and settled on me.

"Mr. Coulter?" he asked.

I nodded and got up, following him back to one of the interrogation rooms. A small desk and a couple of wooden chairs filled the room. A large stand-up ashtray crowded the desk. Anything to make the suspect comfortable.

"Sorry about this," he said, waving around. "This is the only room we have open. Can I get you some coffee?"

I didn't like it. He was being scrupulously polite. When you work with the FBI they're arrogant and superior. When they think they've got something on you they're the model of decorum.

"Sure," I said. He excused himself and left the room. When he came back he was carrying a yellow legal pad along with the coffee. There was another agent with him, a guy about forty or so. Dave wasn't with them. I knew they expected me to ask about him, so I didn't.

"I hope black is okay," he said, setting the cup on the desk in front of me.

"Just fine," I assured him. I took stock of the other

agent. Or at least I assumed he was an agent, but he didn't look it. He was wearing jeans and a short-sleeved shirt that showed a faded tattoo on his left arm. His hair was a wavy light brown, longish. He noticed me looking him over and winked. The agent who had brought me the coffee sat down behind the desk.

"Let me introduce myself," he said. "Special Agent Frank Whitmore." He took out his identification and held it out for me to inspect. Standard procedure. FBI identification cards are about three times the size of an ordinary police ID. Maybe they think that impresses people. Maybe it does. He motioned toward his partner.

"Special Agent Anthony Hill."

The second man waved at me negligently. "Call me Tony," he said. He didn't bother to show me his ID. Whitmore looked over at him, frowning slightly, then settled back in his chair and picked up the legal pad.

"If we could get a few background questions out of the way, just for the record . . ."

"Fire away," I said.

Date of birth? I told him. Place of birth? North Carolina. Married? No. Ever married? No. What kind of car do you drive? 1981 Honda. Color? Gray. It went on like that for a while, with Whitmore making notes, until I started getting annoyed. All the stuff about me was on file, so he was playing some sort of game. Whitmore must have sensed my impatience, since he stopped well short of the full background.

"So," he said, pushing the notepad away, "I understand from Dave Warren that you're the one who found the body of Dodgson, and you think it's connected in some way to the murder of the black kids in Liberty Park."

I nodded.

"How did you know Dodgson was in the shed?"

"I didn't."

"What were you doing there?"

"Just looking around."

"How did you get into the shed?"

I shook my head. "What's the point of all this?"

"Just curious."

I picked up the coffee and took a swallow. It was terrible. I lit a cigarette, leaned back in the chair and crossed my legs. It didn't seem to me Whitmore was all that interested in what I had to say. He had his mind on something else. He waited patiently for me to continue, but I'd played this game before.

Whitmore waited a while longer, then said, "It seems that you have a history of being somewhat . . . impulsive, should we say?"

"I've heard that," I said.

He drummed his fingers on the desk, looked at me without any expression, then opened the drawer of the desk and pulled out an eight-by-ten photo. He slid it across the desk at me. It was a blowup of a picture taken by an automatic bank camera during a robbery. The robber stood there, frozen, staring up at the camera. He was wearing a ski mask, but around the eyes it had slipped down and you could see about a quarter of the face, in three-quarter profile. I examined the photo closely. It showed dark eyebrows, dark recessed eyes, and an angular nose. From what I could see, it did look a little like me. In fact, it looked a lot like me. Shades of Melvin.

"I see," I said. "Where's this from?"

"Union Bank on Fort Union Boulevard," Whitmore said.

"Date?"

"August twelfth. You remember where you were that day?"

"Not offhand."

The other agent, Tony Hill, reached over from his chair and picked up the photo. He held it up in front of his face, looked at me over the top of it, and grinned. "Kind of scary, isn't it?"

"You guys are serious, aren't you?" I said, marveling.

Whitmore laughed, not too convincingly. "No, not really. It's just that a number of people mentioned the resemblance, so we thought we'd ask you about it."

"Sorry," I said. "Much as I'd like to help you out, it isn't me."

"I'm sure it isn't, but you know how it is. We've got to eliminate stuff like this so we can get on with the investigation."

"Sure," I said. "I know how it is."

"Would you be willing to take a polygraph?"

I smiled at him. "I used to be a cop, remember? I know what polygraphs are worth."

"We think pretty highly of them here at the bureau."

"Yeah," I said. "I know you do."

"So, will you take one?"

I shook my head. "Not in this lifetime."

A knowing look came into Whitmore's eyes. Refusal to take a polygraph was as good as an admission of guilt in his book.

"It could save everyone a lot of trouble."

"Yeah," I said, "everyone except me." I stood up and pushed the chair back. "Anything else you want to know?"

Whitmore looked at me for a moment and shook his head. "Tony, sign Mr. Coulter out, will you?"

"Sure thing," the other agent said.

Tony signed me out, but instead of stopping at the door, followed me into the hall.

"I talked to Dave Warren this morning," he said. "He says you think there's some sort of connection between the murder of those two kids and some occult stuff going on."

I shrugged.

"Hey," he said, "don't let Whitmore get to you. We could use some help on this."

I could hardly believe my ears. This guy had just admitted he could use help, and to a civilian at that. You didn't hear that very often. Not only that, he had criticized a fel-

70

low agent, at least by implication. That was totally unheard of.

"Are you really with the FBI?" I said.

He laughed. "A lot of guys around here wonder about that. I was a cop in Dallas for eight years before I joined the bureau. Sometimes I forget myself and still think like a cop. You got time for a cup?"

"Sure," I said. "Why not?"

We ended up at the Roasting Company, right across from the Courts Building on Fourth South. They roast their own coffee and serve fresh-brewed specials of the day. Today it was Costa Rican. I let Tony buy. He was the one who wanted something, though I couldn't figure out quite what yet.

We sat down at one of the outside tables that line the front wall. Two girls who looked like freshmen at the U, real cute, were seated at the next table. Tony glanced at them as we sat down.

"Mmm, mmm," he said. "If only."

"What would you talk about? The relative merits of the Cramps versus the Cure?"

"Talk?" he said, looking at me blankly. I laughed.

We chatted for a while. Tony told me about growing up in Texas. He had a lot of good stories and told them well. He'd never meant to be a cop.

"I wanted to be an English teacher," he laughed. "But right after graduating from the University of Texas, it was straight to Nam. Were you there?"

"I missed it," I said. "Dropped out of school the first year of the draft lottery—my birth date was one of the lucky ones."

"You didn't miss anything, believe me. Anyway, after Nam I came back home, tried to get a job teaching, couldn't, and somehow ended up with the Dallas PD. They were recruiting college grads, trying to upgrade their image. To my surprise I found I liked being a cop. But after eight years it became pretty clear I wasn't going anywhere, so when an opening came up with the bureau I grabbed it."

Tony was good. He was obviously trying to put me at ease. We both knew it. But even so, it worked. He was a likable guy, and I found myself laughing at his stories and throwing in some of my own. With impeccable timing, he picked the right moment to bring up business.

"Okay," he said, "enough of this. You want to know what exactly the hell I want, and why I'm sitting here drinking coffee and trying to convince you what a great guy I am."

"It had crossed my mind."

"Well, it's simple enough, really. See, I'm ambitious. I don't want to spend the next five years in Salt Lake and the five after that in Butte, Montana. I want a promotion, I want to work in Southern California, and you are going to be my meal ticket out."

"I hate to sound stupid, but you just lost me."

"Here's the story. I'm not in such good graces with the powers-that-be at the bureau. About the only way I'm going to get anywhere is to pull off something big, something high profile. The bureau's stuck their neck way out on these murders. Press conference, media releases, the whole thing. Problem is, you've gotta have results. If we screw up, heads roll top to bottom."

"And you're in Butte."

"If I'm lucky. And what worries me is that we're blowing it. Every spare resource is going into the racial thing. The Aryan Nation group up in Idaho, the White Power people in Ogden, skinheads, and anybody else who ever called a black a nigger."

"But you don't think that's it?"

"No, I don't. The whole thing's just too pat. I've got a gut feeling on this that it didn't have anything to do with kids being black. A few years ago I looked into some of these occult groups. They're scary, capable of almost anything. Dave Warren filled us in on this girl you're looking for. Everybody at the bureau dismissed it, but I don't believe in coincidence. I was a cop, remember? This Dodgson guy, and this chick that knew both him and the black kids? Come on. Something's going on here."

"And if you're wrong and it does turn out to be a racial thing?"

"Then I'll bathe in the bureau's reflected glory. I won't be any better off, but I won't be any worse. But if I'm right, and it doesn't have to do with racists, and I come up with the answer . . ."

"Then the other guys are dogshit and you're basking in the Southern California sun."

"You got it."

I looked at him skeptically. "And I'm supposed to make all this happen."

Tony emptied his cup and reached in his shirt pocket for a cigarette. He smoked Camels. I should have known. It fit.

"Well, no, but you could be an awful lot of help. I talked to some people. You were a hell of an investigator before you left the PD."

"They tell you why I left?"

"They told me." He took a drag on his Camel and continued. "Now, there are a lot of things an FBI agent can't do. You know that. Even a street cop has ten times more freedom working a case than I do. The bureau is big on rules, real big. There are a lot of things you can do that I can't."

I nodded. "And just what's your place in this?"

"Information, mostly. I can get you a lot of stuff that's closed off to you now. And don't forget, there are times a federal badge is mighty helpful in getting people to open up."

"True."

"Let me tell you, Jase, we can do it. We can break this

case. You end up with ten thousand dollars reward money and a hell of a rep. I get whatever assignment I want."

I sipped coffee, considering.

"It doesn't hurt to have a friend in the bureau, either," Tony added. "It just might come in useful one of these days."

"Aren't you forgetting a little something?" I said. "Like, your partner thinks I'm a bank robber, for example?"

"Whitmore? Whitmore's got shit for brains. He's got an accounting degree. The only reason he's on you is that you're all he's got. He doesn't have the slightest idea how a real cop does an investigation."

I thought about it for a couple of minutes. You could trust the FBI like a hen can trust a fox. Tony wasn't telling me the whole story, not by a long shot. On the other hand, he didn't seem much like your run-of-the-mill agent. And he was right about one thing—having access to information through the bureau was no small edge. I didn't want to have to bug Dave every time I wanted to find out something.

"Sure, why not?" I said, finally. "What can it hurt?"

I filled him in on where I had gotten so far. Monica, Narada, the Church of the Four-Sided Triangle, and so on. I left a few things out—Brenda's name, Melvin's name, the photos I'd found of Monica in Dodgson's stuff, exactly how I'd got into the self-storage complex—little things. It wasn't just that I didn't trust him completely, it was more that I'd gotten into the habit of never telling anyone everything I knew. A lot of crooks are like that. They'll lie to you even when it's to their advantage to tell the truth. Maybe some of that had rubbed off on me. I did give him the telephone numbers I'd copied from Roger's box of stuff in the basement.

"See who these belong to," I said. "That's about it. Nothing real solid. Also, you said you'd investigated some occult groups. Ever heard of this guy Narada?"

"Not that I recall, but I'll look into him. If he's been into anything anywhere, we'll have something on him in the files." He pulled out a notebook and made a note. "Tell you what, though, there is one guy I'd like to take a good look at. A doctor up by St. Mark's hospital, Leonard Paxton. I heard a lot of stuff about him when I was looking at occult groups. He's a bishop in the Mormon church, very respectable, but rumor had it he was into the occult pretty heavy so I ran a check on him. Arrested in 1972 for Forcible Sexual Abuse. No record of disposition. When I tried to pull the case, the court file turned up missing."

"Who arrested him?"

Tony flipped through the pages of his notebook. "Here it is. Sergeant Don Stovic, Salt Lake City."

"Later Captain Stovic. He retired a couple of years ago. Did you ever talk to him about this Paxton?"

"I got put on a kidnapping that same week. Never got around to it. There wasn't anything specific back then, anyway. But now with this stuff . . ."

"I used to know Stovic fairly well," I said. "I'll look him up. And try some different lines on Monica."

"You think she's hiding out?"

"It sure looks like it. If she does know what's really going on with this shit, she's got to be scared stiff."

Tony took out a card and wrote down a number. "Here," he said, sliding it across the table to me. "Our special hot informant line. You can get hold of me through this after office hours. You'll need a code name."

"I thought the bureau was big on numbers."

"Not for informants. Informants like code names; it makes them feel like James Bond. I've got one right now named Starhawk and another who likes to go by Red Baron."

I considered. "Okay. How about Fred?"

Tony laughed. "Perfect. One more thing, Jase."

"Yeah?"

"If anyone finds out I'm working with you, I can kiss what now passes for my career good-bye."

"Don't worry," I said. "I could say the same thing myself."

THE FIRST THING I DID AFTER TONY LEFT was to call Bob Martin in Burglary. Bob had worked in Dallas before moving to Salt Lake. He and I were still friends, and he still had friends back in Dallas.

"You know anything about Tony Hill?" I asked, after we had traded the usual insults. "A fed, used to work for the Dallas PD?"

"Don't think so. When did he work there?"

"I'm not sure. Probably in the seventies."

"I don't remember him. I left Dallas in 1980. Of course, it's a pretty big department."

"Think you could find someone back there who knew him?"

"Probably. What are you looking for?"

"Nothing specific. Just trying to get a line on what kind of cop he was."

"Call me tomorrow," Bob said. "I'll see what I can turn up."

I got another cup of coffee and sat back down at my table. It was easy enough to tell Tony I was going to be looking for Monica, but this wasn't a simple runaway case anymore. None of the usual lines were going to be much use.

About the only thing I could think of was to follow up the occult angle. Salt Lake is small enough so that anyone seriously into the occult would know at least something about others in the area. I thought for a while longer, and actually came up with an idea. Jan.

I'd met Jan during the time I was having some back problems, the result of getting twisted around by a guy on

PCP I'd tried to arrest one day. She worked as a masseuse out of her apartment, a small sunny place up behind the Capitol. She was Polish, dark haired, pleasant looking, and into shiatsu massage, holistic healing, meditation, nutrition, crystals, the psychic world, witchcraft, and God knows what else. She also removed the pain from my back, so I figured she could believe anything she liked. During our first session, she poked and prodded, then looked seriously at me and pronounced with a slight accent, "You haff a good heart."

I was relieved at having passed her psychic test on my intrinsic worth until she frowned and said, "But your liver—that is not so good. Too polluted. You eat lots of sugar, no?" I had to admit, I ate lots of sugar, yes. She clucked her tongue resignedly and got to work. Jan knew a lot of rather odd people. She might be able to at least point me in the right direction.

An hour later I was stretched out on her massage table appreciating the feel of her hands as she worked on my shoulders and upper back. She put some New Age music on her stereo, something bland and soothing that didn't go anywhere. As she worked I explained what I needed.

"So, you see, I need to find somebody who might know something about these types," I mumbled as she continued to knead.

"Yes, I can see that," she said, leaning on a pressure point. "The problem is, the type of people you want to talk to don't want to talk."

"A common problem in my line of work. Can you think of anyone at all who might be willing?"

She was silent for a while, working down the left side of my back. "Laura McCardle," she said finally. "Laura might know." Another pause. "She knows some of those people. I can call her if you like."

"It would help," I said.

Jan finished up the massage, turned down the music, and picked up a red address book next to the telephone. She dialed a number and carried the phone into her bedroom. I oozed off the massage table and retrieved my clothes. Five minutes later she stuck her head out the door, cradling the phone.

"Laura will talk with you," she said. "I explained what you want. When would be good for you?"

"Now is fine if it's okay with her."

She said something into the phone and nodded, going back into the bedroom. A few minutes later she came out again. She wrote down an address and a phone number and handed it to me.

"What's she like?" I asked, taking it. "Flaky?"

"Flaky? You mean like me?" I started to protest and she laughed, holding up her hand. "It's okay, Jason, I know what you think. You'll like Laura, she's very down to earth. And very pretty."

LAURA'S PLACE TURNED OUT TO BE A small brick house on Wallace Lane, up in Holliday. It was set off the road, secluded from neighbors by a line of poplar trees. Leaves covered most of the yard, and near the house was a plastic bag and a rake giving evidence of a halfhearted attempt to deal with it. I rang the bell and waited for about half a minute before a young woman opened the door.

"Sorry, I'm on the phone," she said, waving me in and motioning toward a couch covered with a red and black spread. She flopped down in the armchair opposite me, sideways, her legs over one of the arms, and picked up the phone.

"Okay, I'm back," she said.

I glanced around the house, not wanting to stare and maybe make her uncomfortable. The main floor was one large room with a high ceiling. A roomy kitchen took up the rest of the floor space. A wood structure, more ladder than staircase, led up to a loft built over the end of the main room. The foot of a king-size bed was barely visible near the edge.

Blankets and rugs covered the walls. Some showed bright colors, others were in dark earth tones. They all featured complex geometrical patterns. At the far end of the room was the obvious reason for this proliferation of coverings: a large loom with a half-finished rug on it.

I turned my attention back to Laura, still talking on the phone. She hadn't seemed to be saying much, just making encouraging noises, interspersed with "I understand" and "Of course." She saw me looking at her and rolled her eyes.

Pretty, Jan had said. More than that, striking. Long blond hair, gathered in back in a barrette, flowed down over one shoulder. Unfashionable for the nineties, but she didn't look like anyone who cared. A squarish face and strong features, a slightly crooked nose and extraordinary mobile lips. She kept making faces into the phone, registering impatience, exasperation, and occasional concern. Baggy black pants and a loose blouse covered her, but she looked solid.

She finally cut off what was apparently an endless monologue from the other end of the phone.

"Jeanne, I've got to go. I've got company. I'll call you back tonight." She listened for another minute. "All right. Love you too. Take care." She put the receiver back on the hook and swung her feet around onto the floor. "My sister," she explained. "Her life isn't going so well."

"It's going around." I waved my hand at the wall hangings. "Yours?"

She nodded. "Mine. I'm a semi-weaver."

"What exactly is a semi-weaver?"

"A weaver who doesn't quite make a living at it. Luckily I have other skills." She sat up straight and wiggled her fingers over an imaginary keyboard. "Temp work. You're Jason?"

I nodded.

She cocked her head to one side and scrutinized me. "Would you like tea? Or some coffee?"

I'd had enough coffee for a while. "Tea would be nice."

She smiled at me. "You don't have to be polite. You're not a tea drinker, I can tell."

"Not usually," I admitted. "It's nice for a change, though."

I followed her into the kitchen and sat down at an old wooden table by the window. She filled a dented copper kettle with water from the tap and put it on the stove.

"Don't worry," she said, unscrewing the top of a jar containing strong-smelling black tea. "No herbal twigs. Plenty of caffeine."

I watched her set out a couple of large mugs and a ceramic teapot. She measured out the tea with quick, deft movements. I don't know what I had expected her to be like, but it was a pleasant surprise. Attractive, I thought. Self-possessed and comfortable. Very attractive.

A scruffy gray cat eased out from behind the refrigerator and eyed me suspiciously, taking a few tentative steps toward me before stopping. It finally decided I was all right and strolled over, rubbing against my leg. Laura sat down across the table from me and stared intently into my eyes. It was a bit disconcerting. Her own eyes were a soft brown.

"Jennifer likes you," she said.

It threw me, and she must have noticed the startled look on my face.

"Jennifer," she repeated, pointing at the cat.

"Oh. She probably smells Stony. My cat."

We talked cats until the tea was ready. She poured it into the mugs and took a sip, holding the mug up to her face and staring at me over the rim of the cup.

"Jan says you're interested in the occult," she said.

"Not exactly. I'm looking for a girl who might be involved with one of the groups."

"Her parents don't approve?"

"Her parents don't seem to approve of very much, but

that's not it. I'm afraid she might be in real trouble. She was with a group called the Church of the Four-Sided Triangle. You know them?"

She nodded thoughtfully. "I've heard of them."

"What kind of stuff are they into? Black magic? Devil worship?"

"Devil worship isn't a very accurate description of anything."

"Well, Satanism, then, or whatever."

Jennifer the cat jumped up into her lap and Laura reached down abstractedly to pet her.

"Do you know anything about Satanism?" she asked.

"Not a whole lot."

"Well, the main thing is that it's basically a power trip. The leaders get off on the power they have over the followers. They're pretty sick, warped. But they can be impressive, too. Charismatic. The followers are mostly total losers, people that life has somehow passed by. They're sad."

"So it's just one more con game, really?"

"No, that's the strange thing. For a lot of people it actually works. That's why it has such a hold on these people. Take some poor slob working at McDonald's. Everybody puts him down. The guys he works with make fun of him. The boss tells him he's a cretin. Then he joins a Satanist group, and the group tells him, No problem—Satan will give you power, make you strong, magically help you. He gets buoyed up with confidence—after all he's got powerful forces on his side. And it shows. It changes his self-image, maybe just a little, but it does change him. People notice, they make fun of him a little less often, maybe treat him with just a little more respect. That reinforces his feelings, and it feeds on itself. Pretty soon he's a total believer. And why not? He's been promised results and he's got them."

"Psychology."

"Most of it. Some strange things do happen, though."

"Like?"

"Oh, nothing that can't be explained by coincidence or the power of suggestion, but even so . . ."

"Sounds pathetic, actually."

"Mostly it is. Anyway, from what I've heard, the Church of the Four-Sided Triangle isn't that much of a group. They aren't really Satanists, even. Sex is their thing. The occult is just an excuse to get it on at orgy time. There are quite a few groups like that. Some guy starts the whole thing up so he can get laid, that's the bottom line."

I flashed on the image of Monica lying stretched out naked on a table. "The guy who runs it is named Narada," I said. "Ever heard of him?"

Laura looked at me strangely, then laughed. She had a nice laugh. "Narada, eh?" She laughed again.

"I'm missing something, aren't I?" I asked.

"Well, if you're looking for Narada, all I can say is that you're on the wrong astral plane."

It took me a moment to get it. "Wonderful," I said. "A pen name."

"I'm afraid so. Narada is a famous name in occult circles. He was supposedly the Manu of Atlantis. What we would call an avatar."

"I see. That's probably why I couldn't find him in the phone book." I drank some tea. "Tell me something, Laura. I don't mean to be rude or anything, but do you really believe in any of this stuff? You don't seem—"

"Weird enough?" She laughed. "Let's just say I like to keep an open mind about certain things."

"Like Satanism?"

"Actually, no. I'm more into things like the Tarot, and self-healing. I've only been to a Satanist meeting once, out of curiosity. Like you said, the people there were pretty pathetic."

"Could they be dangerous?"

"Not the ones I met. Why, do you really think something's happened to this girl?"

"I don't know." I told her a little about Roger and the

kids in the park, and how Monica seemed to be a connection.

"That's terrible," she said, "but I just can't see it. Even if there were some group around I've never heard of, real weirdos, it wouldn't make sense."

"Why not?"

"Well, Satanists, I mean real ones, not what we have around here, believe the whole point of ritual sacrifices is to gain power. The leader of the group gains half the soul, and all the power, of the victim. The other half goes to Satan. And to be truly effective, the victim has to be a willing participant. Shooting down two kids wouldn't make any sense to them."

I got up from the table and stretched. "It doesn't make sense to me either. Nothing about this does. Well, thanks anyway. At least it's given me something to think about."

Laura got up more slowly, letting the cat jump down off her lap, and walked me to the door.

"Jan said you used to be a cop."

"For a while."

"You don't look like a cop."

"Well, that's okay. You don't look like a—"

"Flake?"

I searched for a graceful way out of it. She watched me struggle for a few moments and rescued me.

"Come back sometime," she said, smiling. "I'll do a Tarot reading for you. I've developed a short version for people who think the whole thing's nonsense."

"I just might," I said, and waved a good-bye.

7

It had turned cold as I drove up the canyon. Winter comes early to the mountains. It would be a good while yet before the skiers could hit the slopes, but one monster snowstorm at least was almost a given sometime during October. The clouds looked evil. I was going to have to be careful or one of these days I'd wake up to find my car snowed in for the winter.

Stony was asleep on a chair when I came in and didn't even raise his head. The light on the message machine was blinking. I turned it on and listened to Melvin's thin tones announcing a discovery of earthshaking importance. Meet me at four tomorrow, he said, on the corner by the Stratford Hotel. Make sure you're not followed by you-know-who. One thing I could say about Melvin—at least he liked to do business in the afternoon. There's nothing worse than an informant who wants to meet you at the crack of dawn. I practiced scales on my Gibson for a while, just letting my thoughts drift, hoping something would click. No such luck. I finally gave it up and went to bed.

The next day I stopped next to the post office before

going down the canyon. The snowmobile that came with the cabin was parked there. It needed to be tuned up—track tightened, oil changed, battery checked—all the stuff that's easier to do on a sunny day than in a snowstorm in the middle of the night.

Melvin was busy transacting business inside the hotel foyer when I arrived at the Stratford. I waited until he was done and waved at him. He came bouncing out, rapping at me while he was still a good ten feet away.

"Coulter! Yeah, man, I knew you'd come. I knew you'd show up. I got something, man, I really got something. I knew you'd be here. It's wrapped up, man, I can finger the guy, I can lay out the whole thing, I can—"

"Hold on, guy," I said, grabbing him by the elbow. "Slow down." Melvin was speeding, high as a kite.

"I got an address," he said, reaching in his pocket. He winced as he pulled his arm out, bringing out a crumpled scrap of paper that looked like part of a brown paper bag. He thrust it in my face.

"Here it is, man. This is the place. I got it. This is where that chick Monica used to stay."

I looked at the paper. Melvin's scrawl was indecipherable.

"What does it say?" I asked.

He snatched the paper back from me and held it up. "It's . . . shit, I had it last night. I was kind of out of it, you know, so I wrote it down, so I wouldn't forget it. It's . . . hold on, man, I'll remember . . . 321—no, I got it—271 B Street."

"She still there?"

"I don't think so. The dude I got this from says she split town. Hasn't seen her around."

"You sure about this, Melvin?"

"Dude says he dropped her off there, more than once. And this is where it was."

He held up the paper for emphasis. An angry purple line started at his wrist and traveled up his arm, following the vein. Red streaks shot out across his forearm and it looked hot. I took the scrap of paper.

"What's this?" I asked, holding on to his arm and tracing the line with my fingers.

Melvin shook me off. "Fuck, that's nothin'."

"What exactly have you been shooting up?"

"Just some crank. Nothing heavy. I got it cheap."

"From Terry Winston, right?" I'd seen this before. Melvin got indignant.

"Hey, I ain't no snitch, man. You know that."

"Let's go, Melvin," I said, taking him by the arm again.

"You gonna bust me?"

"Fuck no," I said. "We're going to the hospital."

He tried to pull away. "Oh no."

"What, you wanna die? Don't you know what that shit Terry sells is like?"

"It's speed, man. Righteous crank."

"Yeah?" I said, pulling him along toward my car. "You'll be lucky to keep that arm."

On the way to the hospital I passed by 271 B Street to take a look. It was a red brick house, shades drawn, yard unraked. It didn't look as if anyone was living there.

I took Melvin to Holy Cross. I'd spent so much time there over the last few years most of the staff knew me. The doctor on duty was George Grant, and he took Melvin off to a treatment room while I chatted with one of the nurses. About ten minutes later he came out looking puzzled.

"His arm is badly infected and the whole vein is closed," he said. "What the hell has he been injecting, Jason?"

"Crank," I said. "Methamphetamine. Only, the batch he got is mixed with hydrochloric acid."

"I don't understand. Why would anyone do that?"

"Oh, it's not on purpose," I explained. "The guy he got it from is just a lousy chemist. See, when regular supplies dry up, what some of these guys do is this. They take a nasal inhaler—"

"A what?"

"A nasal inhaler. Originally they all had meth in them, but they phased all of them out except one. Look at the ingredients on the tubes sometime. If you find the right one, you'll see it—it's disguised in chemical jargon, but it's listed right there.

"Anyway, when you get the right type, you break it open, take out the blotter, soak it in a solvent, and then run it through hydrochloric acid fumes. The meth precipitates out. The only trouble is, if you're not really careful, a lot of the HCl gets into the final product."

"And ends up in the arm," said George. "I see. Then the vein shuts down, the arm gets infected, and if it's not treated, turns gangrenous. Then we have a one-armed junkie. What will they think of next?"

"How's our patient?"

"Oh, he'll be all right. We'll keep him a couple of days and hook him up to an IV drip with an antibiotic." George looked at me quizzically. "A friend of yours?"

"Yeah, I guess he is," I said. "But welfare gets the bill."

AFTER I LEFT HOLY CROSS I STOPPED BY POlice headquarters. Salt Lake had acquired a new chief and a new building since I left and the department had gotten security conscious. In the old building, just about anyone could wander in. The new arrangement has a locked access door and a Plexiglas booth protecting the desk officer. All visitors sign in and out. Color-coded badges are the order of the day, different for each floor. I signed in and took the elevator up to six. I stopped by Burglary, looking for Bob Martin. I hadn't been around there for quite a while. A couple of the guys were friendly, a couple pointedly ignored me. Bob was shuffling papers into a briefcase, ready to leave for the weekend. I sat down across from him and lit a cigarette. Bob shook his head and pointed at the NO

SMOKING sign on the wall. Above it loomed a smoke detector, staring out accusingly.

"The whole building is a goddamned nonsmoking zone," he said. "New policy."

I stubbed out the cigarette on the bottom of my shoe and threw it into the wastebasket next to the desk.

"God," I said, "how do you do any work?" Bob was a smoker.

"Who works?"

I looked over at the interrogation room in the back of the office. "What do you do with suspects?" I asked. The timely offer of a cigarette had broken many a case.

"We're trying to figure some way around it. Right now there's a smoke alarm built into the ceiling in each room and they're delicate."

"Take out the batteries."

"They're electronic. Wired right into the main power in the building."

"Progress is a wonderful thing," I said.

Bob gave me a bleak smile. "It's still better than working for a living." He started shoveling more paper into the briefcase. "Well, I got hold of Boo Maycock in Dallas. He used to work with this guy Tony—"

"Boo?"

"Texas, remember? Boo's a good ole boy, but he's no dummy. He worked Robbery with the guy for about a year back in seventy-eight."

"What'd he say?"

"Says he was a good cop. Street smart, pretty level-headed."

"Why'd he join the feds, then?"

"Ambitious. He wasn't going anywhere in Dallas. Seems he had quite a thing for the ladies. According to rumor, he was screwing the captain's daughter and a lieutenant's wife at the same time. Not the best way to play the promotion game."

"Well, the FBI sure isn't the greatest place for a guy who thinks with his dick."

"Maybe he's calmed down since then. Anyway, according to Boo, bottom line is that he was a pretty good cop. Boo says he can be trusted."

When a cop says another cop can be trusted it's a code phrase meaning he won't rat on his partner, no matter what. It doesn't tell you much more than that, but it's not a bad thing to know.

"Many thanks," I said. "Give me a call one of these days. I'll take you out for a cigarette."

THE NEXT STOP WAS DON STOVIC'S HOUSE. I hoped he'd remember the sexual abuse case on Doc Paxton, though 1972 was a long time ago.

Don was quite a character, one of the last of the old breed of cop. He'd grown up in the coal country of Pennsylvania, the only man I ever met who actually said "youse guys" as part of his everyday speech.

I don't think he ever would have retired except for his accident. He was working on his car when the jack slipped and the car landed on his head. Don was tough; he just jacked it back up and kept on working. Finally he noticed there was blood coming out of his ears, so he thought he'd better call 911.

He got fixed up okay, but ever since, whenever he chewed, tears would just pour out of his eyes. I could still see him sitting at his desk with a slice of pizza in his hand, eyes streaming. It got so bad he couldn't eat anything in his car—he couldn't see the road for the tears. He had thirty years on anyway so it wasn't any big thing to retire.

After he retired, Don started growing flowers. He had a greenhouse on the West Side that was his pride and joy. The last time I'd talked to him, it was azaleas that were his passion. He didn't seem to miss police work much.

There was no answer at the front door so I walked

around to the back where the greenhouse was. It was larger than the house, with huge panes of frosted glass. I stuck my head in and yelled his name.

"In back," came his voice. I walked down past rows of green things. The place smelled of wet and dark soil and blossoms. Don came out from behind a bench, trowel in one muddy hand, a sack of peat moss in the other. A little white-haired kindly gardener, squinting up at me. Don had shot five people and killed two of them during his time on the job.

"Ah, a visitor from the world of crime," he said, seeing me. "How goes things at the department, Jase?"

"Well, I sort of retired myself last year."

"Oh? I don't keep up much anymore." He dropped the bag of peat moss and took my arm. "Look at this. Have you ever seen anything so magnificent?" He pointed with the trowel at a bed of red and white flowers.

"Beautiful," I said. "What are they?"

"Jason! Carnations, boy, carnations." He shook his head mournfully. "'What are they?'" he muttered.

Don pulled me to the other side of the aisle. "Roses," he said, gesturing with the trowel again. He peered up at me. "You have seen roses before?"

I admired the roses for a while. Then some begonias. "No azaleas?" I asked.

"Didn't work out," he said shortly. He put down the trowel and wiped his hands on his coveralls. "Well, you didn't come here to admire an old fart's flowers, that's for damned sure. What's on your mind, boy?"

"An old case, one of yours. Thought you might remember something about it."

"Thought you said you retired."

"I get bored," I said.

"Try growing flowers."

"I hate flowers."

Don chuckled. "So what case are we talking about?"

"Leonard Paxton. Forcible Sexual Abuse, 1972. You remember it?"

"Paxton," he said, frowning.

"He's a doctor, if that helps."

"Paxton! That son of a bitch. Yeah, I remember him."

"What was the story?"

Don leaned against a bench with pots on it and took a cigarette from a crumpled pack in the pocket of his coveralls.

"Paxton," he said. "He was a medical student up at the U. Used to dress up and play doctor. See, what he'd do was put on a white coat, slip a stethoscope in his pocket, and wander down to one of the hospitals. He'd go into an examining room, find a young lady, and do a physical on her."

"Including the breasts, I suppose."

"Of course. Not to mention a complete vaginal exam. And rectal. No gloves. Cunt and ass, that was his game."

"How did he get away with it?"

"Well, he didn't for long. Most of the women just figured, well, he's the doctor, and didn't say anything. But one day a lady who was in there for an ear infection got pissed and made a fuss. A real doctor came in, and that was that."

"So what happened to him? The court file is missing."

"That doesn't surprise me any. There was a plea bargain. Paxton agreed to go to counseling, we agreed to drop the charges, med school agreed to let him graduate."

"Gosh. I bet that sure taught him a lesson."

Don lit the cigarette and grinned cynically. "His father is C. Eldon Paxton. The Council of the Twelve?"

"Oh," I said. The Council of the Twelve is as far up as you can get in the LDS church hierarchy. The president of the church is chosen from the council.

"Nothing direct. No orders from above, just subtle pressure. Just let it die." Don took a little short puff on his cigarette and coughed. "Paxton's a member of the Quorum of Seventy himself now."

"Did you ever get to talk with him?"

"Yeah, I did. Weird little duck. Giggled a lot. I asked him just what the Christ he thought he was doing. He said it seemed like a good idea at the time."

"Just another of life's gentlemen. How about his background? Anything weird there?"

"Weird how?"

"I don't know. Occult groups maybe, something like that?"

Don inspected me. "You feelin' okay, Jason?"

"Just fishing."

"Huh. Well, not as I remember. But I guess it could be. I wasn't exactly encouraged to pursue the matter, you know." Don picked up his trowel again. "You ought to spend more time with flowers, you know that?"

"You could be right," I said. "Thanks for the info."

Don nodded. As I walked out of the greenhouse, he yelled after me, "By the way, guess what kind of doctor he became?"

"Don't tell me."

"Yep. A gynecologist."

AFTER I LEFT DON'S GREENHOUSE I DROVE around for a while. The stuff on Paxton was all well and good, but I really was grasping at straws. Maybe Monica was just another scared runaway. Maybe Roger really was a suicide. Maybe I was chasing a very wild goose.

About seven-thirty I headed over to Jimmy's to relax and get a bite to eat. I didn't see anyone I knew, so I slipped into a back booth and ordered a cheese omelet and a Moosehead. Jimmy's wife, Karen, was waitressing, and after she brought the omelet, she sat down for a while to talk. She was on the same kick she'd been on for the last month.

"He's fooling around, Jase, I just know it. I wouldn't mind so much if he'd just be honest and tell me straight out."

"Yes, you would."

"Well, yes, I would. But I can't stand being lied to, either."

I commiserated. "It'll work out," I said, the standard response when there really isn't anything to say.

"Sure it will," she said, and got up to wait on another customer. I went back to the omelet.

I sat in the booth, idly watching the door. A few of the regulars started drifting in. I had just about decided to leave when Laura walked through the door and looked around. She was wearing a loose blouse and a short skirt. Great legs. I waved her over to my table.

"Well, this is a nice surprise," I said, as she walked over. "I didn't know you came to Jimmy's." I motioned toward the booth. "Have a seat."

"Oh, I've been here a few times," she said, sliding into the seat across the table. "A friend of mine's playing tonight. I thought I'd come down and listen."

"Oh. I would have thought you were more into New Age music." She pressed her lips together, started to get annoyed, and then flashed a quick smile instead.

"Stereotyping is a bad idea, don't you think?"

"I do," I apologized. "Sorry."

We talked music for a while. She looked as good as I remembered. I told her I played guitar and sat in once in a while with Kevin, trying to impress her. She expressed some surprise.

"Stereotyping is a bad idea, don't you think?" I said.

She laughed. "Touché."

I finished my omelet. A guy carrying a trumpet case came in and walked over to the booth. He leaned across the table and kissed Laura on the cheek. He had a diamond stud in his left ear. He was young and tall and good-looking. I wasn't too happy about that. He also had a wedding band on his left hand and happened to mention that his wife was coming down later to join him. I suddenly developed a much warmer feeling toward him.

Todd was his name. The other players were setting up so he only had a few minutes to talk, which was fine with me. They played for a while, and he was good, real good. I didn't begrudge him a note.

Laura and I mostly listened, talking between numbers. After Todd finished his set he came over and they talked about people I didn't know. His wife joined us and asked if we wanted to come down to the Green Parrot where some other friends of theirs were playing. Laura looked over at me for a second, and then said no, she was going to go home early tonight. I said the same. After they left, Laura gathered her stuff and looked at me, considering. "You want to come over to my house for a while?"

"Sure," I said. "I'd like that."

"I have to be up early tomorrow. One of the disadvantages of temp work is you work a lot of Saturdays."

I took that as a not so subtle hint. "I won't stay too long," I promised.

A half hour later we were at her place. Jennifer, her cat, sat on the kitchen table between us.

"Tea?" she asked, almost mockingly.

"Tea is fine."

She brewed a pot and poured some for herself as well. Jennifer came over and put her nose in my cup. Laura pushed her off the table and she gave a squawk as she hit the floor.

"Have you had any luck finding your murderous cult?" Laura asked.

"Well, first, it's not my cult. Second, I'm not even sure anymore there's anything to it. It looks like the killer might be a racist crazy after all." I gave her an innocent look.

"You're supposed to be the one with all the arcane knowledge. Any ideas?"

"Tell you what," Laura said, refusing to rise to the bait. "We'll ask the Tarot."

"Will it tell us all?"

"Oh yes. But you probably won't know what it means until long after."

"That's a big help."

She went into the living room and came back with a deck of cards wrapped in silk. She pulled them out and spread them face up on the table, separating out what looked like face cards. They were old and worn, double headed.

"A Piedmont deck," she said. "I'm a traditionalist. First, choose a significator, a card that represents you. Traditionally, older men who have reached a degree of wisdom choose a King. Younger men usually choose a Knight."

I looked at the cards on the table. Four men on horseback, one with a helmet and beard carrying a sword; one holding up a disk; one a cup; and one carrying what looked to be a tree limb crossed with a beefsteak. It intrigued me.

"This one," I said, picking the tree limb.

"Knight of Wands. Interesting."

"That's what psychiatrists say when you tell them your girlfriend reminds you of your mother."

"I would have thought Swords would be your choice. Wands are more intuitive, less direct. Impetuous, though, not always thinking things through."

"Couldn't be me," I said.

She gathered the rest of the cards, shuffled them thoroughly, and cut the deck.

"I'll do a very basic layout, just five cards. Give me a number between one and twenty-two."

"Nine."

She counted cards, put the ninth face down to the left of the Knight, shuffled, and cut again.

"Another number."

"Five."

This one went to the right. The next went above, the next after that below, and the last card on top of the Knight.

"The first card represents what the situation is at the present, the driving force, so to speak."

She turned it over. A man with a hat holding something in one hand stared at me. *Il Bagatto,* the card read.

"The Juggler," she said. "Sometimes called the Magician. The manipulator. The master of illusion. But more than that, it represents control over things—or at least the desire for control."

I grunted noncommittally. She put her fingers on the second card. "This crosses you. Obstruction, negative influences, problems." She turned it over.

"King of Cups. A court card usually represents a person. The King of Cups is a powerful and focused individual. Usually respectable on the outside, but inside, violent, secretive, twisted, and utterly without conscience."

"Ahh," I said. "Narada rears his ugly head. You sure that's not a cold deck?"

"Discussion," she said, turning the next card. "What comes from the conflict. Eight of Wands. A card of movement, speed, things coming to a head, perhaps too fast."

"More like going around in circles, if you ask me."

She shrugged. "Synthesis next. That which results from the other factors."

The card she turned over depicted two dogs baying at the moon. Behind them were some hills and buildings. The card gave me the creeps. Laura's mouth turned down. "The Moon. Paranoia. Deception. Hidden enemies and false friends. Not a good card, especially there." She looked up. "It may mean that things are not what they appear."

"Are they ever?"

Laura started to turn over the last card. I put my hand over hers to stop her.

"Wait a minute," I said. "I've seen this script. You turn over the last card and there it is, staring up at you: Death."

She looked at me with tolerant amusement. "You should be so lucky. Last card is solution, probable outcome."

She turned it over deliberately. It had an odd wickerlike design with two ornate swords crossed over the center. Laura stared at it, drumming her fingertips on the table.

"Well?" I said.

"Not well, actually. Ten of Swords. To put it bluntly, the worst card in the deck. Death. Ruin. Disaster. The failure of all plans. The ending of all hopes."

"How cheerful. Very encouraging."

She gathered the cards together and mushed them up, obviously upset. "The Tarot doesn't really foretell the future, you know. It only shows what may be, probabilities, trends."

"Don't worry," I said. "I'll keep my eyes open."

We sat in silence for a while. Laura evidently took the cards more seriously than she let on. Jennifer the cat jumped back on the table, stepping on the cards. We both started stroking her abstractedly and I naturally progressed to lightly stroking Laura's arm. She looked at me and smiled, then gave herself a little shake.

"It's getting late," she said, "and the firm of Beeson and Walters desperately needs a warm body tomorrow morning. A body that can type."

"Far be it from me," I said, rising to my feet, "to deprive them of your services."

Laura walked me to the door and opened it. I stood there a moment facing her and put my hands on her shoulders. She rested her hands on my waist, so I kissed her. It was nice. She reacted without hesitation, her mouth warm, her tongue sweet and responsive. After a while I stepped back and looked at her questioningly.

"Never on the first date," she said.

"I've seen you twice, now."

"Beeson and Walters," she said. "It's midnight. I get up at six."

"I don't mind."

"I do." She leaned forward and gave me a quick kiss on the cheek. "Call me," she said.

I DROVE AWAY FEELING SMUG. THE CARDS might forecast ruin, but right now a nice lady was just what I needed to perk up my life. Nothing heavy. Just something nice. I thought about Jennifer. The person, not the cat. Maybe Portland was a good place for her.

I wasn't quite ready to go home. On impulse I pulled over and called police Dispatch.

"Wanda?" I said, recognizing the voice that answered. "This is Coulter."

"Jason! Boy, it's been a long time. What have you been up to? And why haven't you been by to see me?"

"I thought you were living with Barstow."

"God, you *are* out of touch. That's been months."

"Oh."

"Never mind. You'll be sorry."

"Wouldn't be the first time. Listen, who's working two-one-five?"

"Ronnie Jamison, I think." Ronnie was an old friend from patrol days.

"Can you get hold of him for me?"

"Just a sec, I'll see." She altered her tone to a cool professional radio voice. "Two-one-five, check."

I could hear his response from the speaker over the phone.

"Two-one-five, Sixth South, Sixth East."

"Ten-twelve for a message."

Wanda spoke back into the phone. "What do you want me to tell him?"

"If he's not busy, have him meet a party at nine and four in about ten minutes."

I heard him acknowledge, told Wanda thanks, and headed down to the Village Inn on Ninth East and Fourth South, one of the few late night coffee shops on the East Side. It was getting cold and had started to rain. We might even get some snow on the benches before the night was over. I waited in the parking lot out front until Ronnie arrived.

"Jason," he said, opening the passenger door and clearing his junk off the seat beside him. "Well, I'll be damned."

"Not much doubt of that," I said, sliding into the passenger seat.

"What you been up to, big guy?"

"Not much. Looking for a girl."

"Aren't we all, though?" Ronnie was recently divorced. "You know how you can tell when you're really hard up? It's when you come off graveyard shift, turn on the Saturday morning Flintstones cartoons, and find yourself seriously considering whether Wilma or Betty would be better in bed."

I laughed and took out a cigarette. "Bum me one of those, will you?" Ronnie said. I flipped another up out of the pack and he leaned over and took it. "You want to ride for a while? It's been pretty dead for a Friday."

"Sure," I said. We cruised around for a while, talking old times, checking the back alleys and side streets. The radio was silent. The only sound was the rain falling and the hiss of tires on the street.

"So who's this girl?" he finally asked.

I showed him a photo of Monica and gave him an edited version of why I was looking for her.

"You working two-one-five all month?" I asked. Liberty Park was included in 215.

"Until November first. You want me to keep an eye out for her?"

"If you would." I lit another cigarette as we turned into an alleyway. "Tell me, Ron, how long has it been since you were active in the church?"

"I don't know, couple of years. Why?"

"You know anything about a guy named Paxton? Leonard Paxton? Member of the Quorum of Seventy?"

"I know the name. I don't know much about him. Why, is he mixed up in something?"

"I don't really know. He might be, but it seems a bit far out."

"Well, if it's far out, the church is as good a place to look as any. Mormons are basically a cult, you know."

"Right." After his divorce, Ronnie had dropped out of the church. Now he had a real thing about it.

"No, really. They are."

"It's not quite the same, Ron."

"No? If there were five thousand of them in the world instead of five million, people would be shouting 'Moonie' at them in the streets."

"Oh, come on. Mormons aren't all that different from Catholics or Protestants, except for the occasional polygamist."

"Oh, really? Tell me, Jase, you know where the Book of Mormon comes from? Joseph Smith translated it from some Golden Plates he found, using the 'Urim and Thrummin'—magic spectacles given to him by an angel. That doesn't sound just a wee bit peculiar?"

"Well . . ."

"And how about this? American Indians are really descendants of the lost tribes of Israel. Or this. You know why Mormons have so many kids? It's a duty. You see, they have to provide homes for disembodied spirits from a preexistent life."

"Well . . ."

"And get this. When you die, if you've been a good boy, you get to become an actual god yourself—with your own private universe to play with. And populate. Why do you think they needed all those wives? Sound like mainstream Christianity to you?"

"No, but it sounds pretty damn good, actually," I said.

"Two-one-five." The radio squawked, breaking the quiet.

Ronnie picked up the mike. "Two-one-five."

"Two-one-five, 'Woman screaming,' 452 South 500 East. Anonymous complainant. NFD."

NFD. No further details. When you work patrol, the most common words in the language. Before Ronnie could respond another voice cut in.

"Two-one-seven. That's just the Koslows at it again. I'll take it. I'll advise on a back."

"Ten-four. Two-one-five, copy?"

"Copy."

Ronnie put back the mike and grinned at me. "Ah, the wonder and excitement of police work," he said. "You ever miss it?"

"Sometimes. Not that stuff, though."

We drove around for a while longer shooting the shit, then Ronnie dropped me off at my car, promising again to keep an eye out for Monica. I headed up the canyon, and halfway up, the rain started turning to sleet. I thought I might even have to take the snowmobile up to the cabin, but the snow tapered off and stopped before I reached Alta. I was yawning as I climbed the cabin stairs, and had a good night's sleep for the first time all week.

8

I was already up when Tony called late in the morning.

"Did you get the story on Paxton?" he asked.

I told him what Stovic had told me.

"So. This guy might turn out to be very interesting," he said. "I've got to go up north to interview one of those White Power types, but just maybe I'll stop by his office on the way and have a talk with the good doctor. You interested?"

"Of course," I said. "You sure he's there on a Saturday?"

"I called. He's there till one. The office is in that medical building right across from St. Mark's."

"I'll be there in half an hour," I said.

Just before noon we walked into the office together and told the receptionist we were there to see Dr. Paxton.

"Did you have an appointment?" she asked, eyeing us doubtfully.

Tony took out his badge and showed it to her, confidentially, shielding it from the patients in the waiting room.

"I'll tell him you're here," she said, somewhat flustered. FBI badges do get results. She disappeared into the back and we took a seat in the waiting room. A teenage girl and her mother were sitting across from us, half hidden by a huge potted plant situated on a table in the middle of the room. The girl stared at us through the fronds, then giggled and whispered something to her mother. The mother looked at her disapprovingly and went back to her magazine.

"What do you think?" asked Tony. "Good-guy, bad-guy?"

"Depends on how dumb he is. Let's play it by ear."

The receptionist came back in and motioned to us. "The doctor can see you now," she said.

Paxton's small office had the usual framed certificates and medical books. Papers were slopped untidily on his desk. There was just room for two chairs across from it.

He was sitting behind the desk when we came in, a plump, pink, balding man in his early forties. The office was overheated, and the few strands of hair he had left straggled limply across his scalp. He bounced to his feet and held out his hand. "Leonard Paxton," he said, and giggled.

Tony showed him his ID and we all sat down.

"Well, well, the FBI," he said. He had a high squeaky voice. "I hope I haven't done anything naughty." He giggled again.

"Like what?" said Tony, throwing him on the defensive right away.

Paxton turned bright red. He stammered and looked over toward me for help. The old good-guy, bad-guy routine has been done to death, but Paxton looked like he would buy anything. I shook my head reassuringly.

"Nobody thinks you did anything, Doctor. We just have a few questions, thought you might be able to help us."

He relaxed. Tony, of course, jumped him immediately. He pulled out his notebook and made a show of looking through it.

"Forcible Sexual Abuse, 1972. Would you care to tell us about that, Doctor?" He stressed the "Doctor," making it sound like some loathsome lower life form.

"That was a very, very long time ago," Paxton said, darting a quick tongue over his lips. "I don't see what—"

"What about lately? You been a good boy? Does the name Narada mean anything to you, for instance?"

"Narada?" He looked over at me for help, but this time I didn't give him any.

"Well, how about the name Monica, then?" I said. "As in Monica Gasteau, for example."

That shook him. "I . . . I'm . . ."

"She knows you, Doctor. She knows you very well."

Paxton's response surprised me. He stared at us without speaking for about ten seconds and then suddenly buried his face in his hands. After a moment he straightened up.

"It's absurd. To begin with, she's a pathological liar."

"Oh? She seemed pretty believable to me," I said.

"You don't know her." He gave off another squeaky giggle.

"Where did you meet her?" Tony asked. "Was she a patient, or was it at one of your weird rituals?"

Paxton looked at me, then over at Tony, then back to me. He looked confused. And he looked worried.

"Just exactly what is this about?" he asked.

I leaned forward and regarded him thoughtfully. "You tell me, Doctor."

"This isn't a fucking game anymore," Tony put in. "We're talking murder now."

I shot a quick glance at Tony. Bringing up the subject of murder was a bad mistake. I was surprised; Tony was supposed to be an experienced investigator. Sure enough, Paxton stiffened.

"I don't . . . I don't think I want to talk anymore. I don't have to, you know. I think maybe I'd better consult my attorney before this goes any further." He stood up behind his desk.

"That's your privilege," Tony said, getting up himself. "But next time we talk, Doctor, it'll be just a bit more formal."

Paxton was on the phone before we got out of the door. Once outside, Tony looked at me and nodded.

"Yep. I think we just might have something here."

"Maybe." I lit a cigarette and took a deep drag. "Talking about murder right off the bat wasn't such a hot idea, you know."

Tony shook his head. "No, you're wrong there, Jase. We might as well rattle his chain and see which direction he jumps. He knew he was in deep shit the minute we walked in."

"Maybe," I said again.

"Fuck, it doesn't matter one way or the other anyway. If he's our man, and I think he just might be, we'll make him on it sooner or later."

"You think so?"

"I know so. Look, first of all, he's into the occult, right? Remember, I tied him into that long before any of this happened. Second, he's a pervert, on record. Third, did you see what the name Monica did to him?" Tony lapsed into a deep Texas accent. "Man, he was shakin' like a dog shittin' peach pits."

"Maybe," I said for the third time. "Can you really see him lying in a vacant lot with a three-oh-three rifle?"

"Well, no, to be honest, not really. But he's into this shit up to his ass. Hell, I'd stake my career on it. He didn't have to do the killings himself, you know." Tony hesitated, then changed the subject. "You want to get some firsthand knowledge on what these people are really like?"

"What do you mean?"

"I talked to one of my old snitches today. There's a

group that's having a gathering tonight out west of Riverton. I thought we'd go take a look at them."

"They let anyone just walk in?"

"I know the place. We can get a good view without getting too close. Bring some field glasses. They'll get started about dusk, so meet me at the south end of Valley Fair Mall about six. We'll get there early and set up." He looked at his watch. "Gotta run. You game for tonight?"

"Sure," I said. "Why not?"

I SPENT THE REST OF THE AFTERNOON IN the library going through their occult section. I found out a lot of interesting things, but nothing that helped. Everything I read confirmed what Laura had suggested—that from an occult standpoint, the murders didn't make any sense. And I just couldn't see the rotund Leonard Paxton as an archvillain in any case.

Monica could have well been a patient of his, though. So, given his predilections, maybe he'd done a little something out of line. Then I remembered. Monica's father had said something about her being involved with a high school teacher. And then something about a doctor. I made a quick call to the Gasteau house.

"A doctor?" Marie Gasteau said after I asked her. "Oh, well, that was just more of her wild accusations." She lowered her voice confidentially. "Monica is just obsessed with sex, you know."

"What exactly did she say?"

"It's really not important. I mean, what does it have to do with finding her?"

"You never know. Who was the doctor?"

She hesitated. "Dr. Paxton," she said. "Dr. Leonard Paxton. He's a very nice man, really. I do hope you're not going to cause any trouble for him."

"Not if I don't have to," I said.

That made things clearer. The good doctor had slipped up again. With his background he'd make a good target for a spot of blackmail. No wonder her name upset him so.

This wasn't getting me any closer to finding out who killed the two kids, though. I drove out west to the Valley Fair Mall, getting there just after six. Tony was parked at the south end, and held open the passenger door as I parked next to him.

"Jump in," he said. "You bring binoculars?"

I got a pair out of my bag in the trunk, threw them in the backseat, and climbed in next to Tony.

"So, where are we headed?"

"Not too far. It's kind of out of the way and hard to find, though."

We headed south. Tony was whistling, in a good mood. I appraised him carefully.

"You know," I said, "I think you really get off on this stuff."

"The occult? No, not really, most of it's bullshit, but there are things . . ."

"Like what?"

"Oh, you know. Things."

He didn't say anything else for a couple of minutes, then turned his head slightly and looked at me out of the corner of his eye.

"Jase, haven't you ever had anything happen to you that you just can't explain rationally?"

"Lots of times. Mostly they have to do with women."

"No, I'm serious."

"Okay. Such as?"

Tony shrugged, embarrassed. "Well, for instance, when I was a kid. My mom and dad split up for a while and Mom took me back to Vermont for the summer. We lived out in the middle of nowhere, in an old barn her folks had converted into a summer home. My bed was up in what used to be the hayloft."

"Pretty neat for a kid."

"Yeah, I thought it was. There was another house about half a mile back down the dirt road, another family with a kid my age, Charlie Crystal."

"How old were you?"

"Shit, I don't know, six, maybe seven. We got to be best friends, which wasn't surprising since there wasn't anyone else around. We'd go off together, explore the woods, all that kid stuff. Except, there was one section of the woods neither one of us would go into. We were scared shitless of it."

"A lot of kids are scared of the woods."

"Not me, not even at night. Anyway, it wasn't the woods, it was just this one section. Charlie and me started making up stories about it. And the one that stuck, the one that became it for us was this: Something bad lived there—something large, and dangerous, and horrible. Not an animal, a 'something,' something we talked about in whispers because it wasn't a very good idea to draw its attention to you. It was huge and flew over the tops of the trees. And here's the kicker—if it called you by name and you heard it calling, you had to go with it. Forever."

"You and Stephen King," I said. "Quite an imagination you had."

"Sure. Only, when I was in college, taking an anthro course, I ran across that exact same story. I mean word for word. Apparently it's a pretty common Indian legend, especially typical in the Northeast. The Indians had a name for this thing we made up. They call it the Wendigo. That's also the name they gave to people who eat other people. And their story of the Wendigo is exactly the same as what we made up, two little kids off in the middle of nowhere. So, you explain that."

"You got any Indian blood?" I said lightly.

"As a matter of fact, I do. A great-grandfather on my mother's side."

He started to say something else and changed his mind. I looked out the window for a while. We had reached the

108

south end of the valley, where Salt Lake gradually turns from urban to suburbs to hard-core rural. Thirty minutes from downtown Salt Lake City, horses and cows graze in the fields. Broken-down farmhouses abound, unidentifiable machinery rusting in the front yards. Signs for McDonald's give way to BEEF SIDES—HALF OR WHOLE.

To the west, the farms become more widely scattered and the fields of crops become sparser. The brown earth turns gray, then sandy, as the desert intrudes. Near the foothills that border the western side of the valley the green things have given up, and only sand dunes remain stretching out into a stark lunar landscape.

About a mile from the hills a dirt track led off the main road. Dozens of fresh tire tracks led up over the crest of a hill, leaving no doubt we were in the right place. We drove another half mile to where the road curved around, pulled off the road, and scrambled up the hill from the other side. It was getting dark by the time we got set up, but there was still enough light to see.

On the other side of the hill, at the bottom, about thirty cars were parked. Most of the people standing around were men, but there were a few women as well. As it grew darker they started drifting off in twos and threes toward a flat area where someone had started a large bonfire.

"Looks like a good crowd tonight," Tony said. He took a pair of unwieldy binoculars out of the daypack he was carrying and raised them to his eyes. I got out my own and focused on the fire. It's hard to see much in dim light with binoculars. The magnification was fine, but it was like looking out a window at night, trying to see something across the street when the streetlight is out. Large, dim shapes kept flitting through the field of vision.

"This isn't going to work," I said. "I can't see a fucking thing."

Tony smiled knowingly and reached back into his pack. "Try this."

He handed me a short telescope. On the side of the

scope it read, *Sigma XQ*. It was a starlight scope. Starlight scopes gather about ten times the light as conventional telescopes. They also cost about ten times as much. Working with the FBI does have some advantages. Starlights are light gatherers, not true infrared scopes, the ones that will work in total darkness, but they work fine in something like moonlight. The light given off by the fire was more than enough.

I focused in again, and this time it was like being right there. They seemed to be getting down to business. Somebody had turned up a boom box and the sounds of heavy-metal music echoed up toward us. A dark-haired man was drawing something in the sand a little away from the fire. He looked pretty ordinary.

"What, no robes?" I said, a bit disappointed.

"Movie stuff," said Tony. "I recognize that guy, though, the one drawing the pentagram. He's a total psycho in real life."

"As opposed to right now," I muttered. Two other guys were setting up what looked like a portable altar, sort of a long picnic table covered in black velvet. The whole scene struck me as more tacky than evil. When they turned toward the fire I got a look at their faces. The one on the right was Leonard Paxton, M.D. Tony grunted, seeing him at the same time.

"Just an innocent little babe," he said quietly.

After a while they seemed to have everything ready. The group gathered around the makeshift altar, more purposeful now. I scanned the crowd, looking for Monica, but none of the women looked familiar. The guy who had been drawing in the sand faced the group, held up his arms until there was silence, and started a high-pitched chant. After a while the group began to answer in a call-and-response. At first it was funny, like a bad made-for-TV movie, but as they got more into it, the replies became more frenzied and real. The whole thing had a nasty, ugly undertone to it.

Finally the leader held up his arms again and there was

silence, expectant this time. Paxton walked up to the altar carrying a cloth sack that squirmed as he set it on the table. He undid the top of the sack, reached in, and brought out what was inside.

It was a small black cat, and it crouched on the table, the tip of its tail jerking nervously. Paxton stroked it with small pudgy hands, apparently trying to soothe it. The leader intoned something short and the group responded with a shout. The cat bolted and almost made it off the table, but Paxton caught it with one of his fleshy hands. It rolled over on its back in surrender. It must have been somebody's pet to be so docile. No wild cat would give up so easily. Paxton reached out with his other hand, and someone stepped up and placed a kitchen knife in his outstretched palm.

"This is really sick," I said.

"No shit," Tony replied.

Paxton showed the knife to the crowd, hesitated a dramatic moment, and then rapidly brought the knife down to the throat of the cat and pulled it across with a jagged motion. The cat doubled up and Paxton quickly let go, not wanting to get clawed. I felt sorry that the cat hadn't even managed to get one lick in. It pulled itself up on its front legs and tried to get to its feet, but couldn't quite make it. It swayed for a few long moments and then toppled over on its side, curled up in a ball, and lay there unmoving. There seemed to be a lot of blood for such a small cat. Paxton picked up the limp body and held it high. There was an approving murmur from the crowd. He unceremoniously tossed it aside and there was another murmur as the crowd awaited the next act.

From somewhere in the back of the crowd a young woman appeared wearing a tattered bathrobe. She wasn't particularly attractive, but had thick, long dark hair. She approached the altar and shrugged out of the robe, letting it fall to the ground. Not surprisingly, she was naked underneath. She climbed up onto the table and stretched out, unconcerned with the blood that was still soaking the fabric. As she lay down I could see her face clearly. She was vacant eyed and smiling. Paxton walked over to the dark-haired man and handed him the knife.

"Hey," I said. "This is getting a little out of hand."

Tony didn't say anything. The dark-haired man walked up to the altar and raised the knife high. He said something in a tone that rose at the end, apparently asking a question. Whatever it was, the assembled group responded with a resounding affirmative, and he brought down the knife in a swift plunge, so quick it caught me by surprise. The woman arched and uttered a heartrending scream.

"Jesus Christ," I said, half scrambling to my feet. Tony grabbed me by the arm and pulled me back down.

"Too late, Jase," he murmured.

I picked up the scope again and trained it on the scene below. My hands were shaking. The dark-haired man had thrown the knife down by his feet and was bending over her. He appeared to be kissing her on the breasts. Then he rolled her over and began frantically tugging at his belt, trying to get his pants off. I was just about to be sick when I noticed that the woman had shifted slightly, as if to get more comfortable. The man, naked now from the waist down, climbed up on the table and roughly jerked the woman's rear up in the air, so she was resting on her knees with her face pressed into the table. She stayed in that position while he quickly mounted and entered her. He began thrusting vigorously, and I could see the woman was cooperating.

"Best porno show in the valley," Tony said, poking me in the ribs.

"He didn't really stab her," I said, stupidly stating the obvious.

"Nah, it's just symbolic. First the cat, then the phony human sacrifice, then they fuck."

"You motherfucker, you've seen this before."

"A couple of times. Kind of gets you the first time, don't it? Look, he's finished already. Let's see who's next."

The dark-haired man was climbing off, to be replaced by Paxton. The good doctor went at it with a fervor that surprised me, considering his tubby little physique. He was finished as quickly as the first man, and someone else took his place. I took the scope from my eye and blinked at Tony.

"These people are killers?" I asked skeptically.

He put down his binoculars and reached for a cigarette.

"You bet," he said. "They do this kind of thing all the time, but every once in a while they find a girl without any connections—a runaway, someone from out of state, something like that. She comes to a few of their little orgies, gets invited to be the guest of honor, thinks it's a real kick. Only, this time they actually go through with it."

"And you just watch?"

"No, of course not. They're very careful when they do a real one. But I've heard about it, from more than one source." He picked up his binoculars again. "Still think Doc Paxton is a harmless little pervert?"

We watched until the group turned into a full-fledged orgy and then walked back down the hill to the car. I didn't say much on the way back. I was thinking. Tony pulled up next to my car and turned in the seat to face me.

"What say we talk to the doctor again, soon?"

"Might be a good idea," I admitted. "By the way, you get anything yet on those phone numbers I gave you?"

"Sorry, no. I've been too busy to get back to the phone company."

"Got something else for you, while you're at it. An address."

"Shoot," said Tony, pulling out a small notebook.

"Two-seventy-one B Street."

"Who lives there?"

"That's the question. Not just who owns the place, it might be rented. Try Mountain Fuel and Utah Power and Light. See who pays the bills."

"Hey, good thought, Jase. I would never have come up with that on my own. See, I've only been a cop for fifteen years."

"Sorry," I said.

"No problem," Tony laughed, as he drove off. "I'll get back to you."

9

When I woke up the next day, I realized a week had gone by since the killings. Not a good sign—if you don't develop some pretty strong leads in the first forty-eight hours, you probably never will. I called Dave at home but got no answer. I puttered around the house for a while, picked up Jennifer's letter and stared at the phone number a couple of times, and finally decided to take a long hike to clear my mind.

I pushed it all the way up Superior Ridge, and by the time I got back to the cabin, my legs were dead. My mind wasn't noticeably clearer, but it was blank enough with fatigue to serve the purpose. At least I'd have no trouble catching up on lost sleep. Tomorrow I could drop by the homicide division and see if they'd come up with anything new.

When I walked into Homicide the next afternoon, Dave was seated at his desk, on the phone. I perched myself on the corner of the desk and waited. Mike Volter stuck his head out of his office and saw me. He scowled, but didn't say anything. Dave hung up the phone and pumped his arm like Karl Malone after a monster dunk.

"We're on to something, Jase," he said. "We might have him."

"What have you got?" I asked, feeling a mild twinge of disappointment. I had sort of started feeling it was my case, not the department's.

"A hooker. Maggie May, that's her street name." Dave tossed an old mug shot across the desk at me. A rather plain, plump girl with long straggly hair looked up at me.

"She came in this morning," said Dave, "and told us quite a story. About a week ago, she's standing at Fourth South and State. A guy pulls up in a Camaro, a nice car, she says, with out of state plates. She walks up to the car, goes through the usual routine, and then gets into the car with him. As soon as she's in the car, the very first thing this guy asks is, 'Have you got a nigger for a pimp?' She tells him no. 'Do you date niggers?' She says no again. She does, but she tells him what he wants to hear. Now get this, you know what the very next thing he asks is?"

"What?"

"'Is there a nigger pimp in town I can kill for you?'"

I settled myself a little more comfortably on the desk. "A nice friendly offer."

"Yeah. Of course, being a working girl, she doesn't need any hassle, so every time he alludes to blacks, she says, 'Yeah, I hate niggers, too,' or something to that effect. They get together on a price, and she takes off with him.

"They don't go to a motel right away, though. This guy seems to want some company, so they drive around for a while looking for somewhere to eat. They go to a couple of drive-ins, but he has to drive through and make sure there are no black cooks or black employees. He won't eat food if it is prepared or served by blacks."

"I'm beginning to get the idea this guy doesn't care much for black people."

116

"Sharp, Jase, very sharp. Anyway, they stop at a light at Seventeenth and State and this black dude walks in front of the car. Our guy takes out what sounds like a three fifty-seven, draws a bead on the guy and says, 'Should I kill him? Should I kill him?' Maggie just freaks out. 'No, no, don't do it. Please.' Shit like that. Finally, he puts the gun away."

"You think he was serious or just fucking with her?"

"Maggie seems to think he meant it. She's a junkie, of course, but she's been around for a while. Eventually they end up at a trick house and screw."

"Kinky?"

"No, she says he just wanted it straight. Afterwards, she asks if he can take her home. He says fine, and as they're driving over to her apartment, he starts talking about killing blacks again.

"'I've killed niggers before,' he says. 'It's no big deal. The way you do it is, you always do it from a distance. That way, when they fall, all the attention is directed to them, and that gives you an opportunity to get away. So you never just go up and shoot them directly. You always do it from a distance.'

"He talks some more along these lines, but Maggie's not really listening too close. She just wants to get home, shoot up, and watch some TV."

"There's a lot of money being offered for this one," I said. "Why'd she wait till now?"

Dave shrugged. "Hey, Maggie's a street whore. Most of them don't even know what day it is, and Maggie's no exception. She doesn't read newspapers, she doesn't watch TV news. She didn't even know anyone had been killed until a friend of hers told her about the reward. She almost didn't come in anyway, just thought it was a weird coincidence, but the money got to her."

"So you think this guy is really good for it?"

Dave gave me a disgusted look. "What do you want, an eyewitness?"

"And how does he tie in with Monica, and Debbie in the hospital, and Roger sitting in his VW?"

"What? Oh, your occult stuff. Sorry, Jase, you're way off on that. Sure, there's something weird going on there, but it doesn't have anything to do with this. Hey, look at this guy. He drives a Camaro. He hates blacks. He claims he goes around killing blacks. He comes into town and two black kids are shot down for no apparent reason. That's a lot of coincidence."

"He does look good," I admitted. "Did you get a name?"

Dave shook his head.

"Who interviewed Maggie?"

"Becker."

I didn't say anything. I didn't have to. We both knew how many cases Becker had fucked up with his attitude. I wasn't ready to give up quite yet.

"What about Roger?" I asked. "What does the medical examiner say?"

"Inconclusive. Still officially a suicide."

"Inconclusive? That's a lot of help. What exactly did he say?"

Dave gave a resigned grunt. "Be my guest," he said, picking up the phone and dialing the M.E.'s office.

"Terry Kirkland, please," he said into the receiver. A pause. "Terry? Dave Warren. Somebody wants to talk to you." He handed me the phone.

Terry was surprised to hear my voice. "I thought you were gone from there," he said.

"I still drop by every now and then. I got some questions on Roger Dodgson. The guy in the Volkswagen?"

"Oh, yeah. Shoot."

"What did he die from?"

"Hard to say with a body that old. No external trauma that I could find. Probably CO, carbon monoxide, since there was a high concentration in the spleen, but it's not conclusive."

"How about drugs?"

"Well, he shot up sometime before he died. Interesting, though, high heroin, very low morphine."

"Which means?"

"Well, he could have died from an OD."

"But it's not conclusive."

Terry laughed. "See, here's the thing. When someone shoots up, the body metabolizes the heroin and turns it into morphine. If the guy shot up a few hours before death, you'd find maybe a little heroin and a lot of morphine. If he shot up and OD'd instantly, you'd have all heroin and no morphine."

"I see. And if somebody else shot him up with enough to put him in a coma and he died from it say, half an hour later, you'd have some metabolization but not that much—high heroin and low morphine."

"Exactly. Just the same as you'd get if he fixed right there in the car, then died soon after from the CO coming out of the exhaust."

"Any guess on which is the more likely?"

"No way to tell, really. Sorry."

Just like Dave said. Inconclusive.

THERE WASN'T ANY POINT IN TRYING TO discuss the occult angle with Dave for a while. He was too hot for this new lead. Maybe he was on the right track after all. It was too bad Becker had been the one to interview Maggie May. She might have had a lot more to say to someone else.

I considered it. Maggie wouldn't be too hard to find, if she was working State Street. Hookers never tell the cops all they know; they always hold *something* back. She might be more willing to talk to someone who wasn't a cop. Especially if that someone could provide an incentive.

I checked my wallet. I still had the black tar heroin from

Roger's basement. Not too bright of me to be carrying it around, come to think of it.

It took an hour of cruising up and down State Street before I spotted Maggie leaning against the pawnshop on the corner of Fourth. She was better looking than her picture, thinner, and she had cut her hair shorter. I drove by slowly, giving her the eye, letting her see me looking her over. I circled the block, drove by her again, and pulled over to the curb on the third circuit. She shoved herself away from the building and came over to the car. I leaned over and rolled down the passenger window.

"Hi," I said. "How ya doin'?"

She looked me over carefully. "Hi," she said. "You looking for a date?"

"Could be. How much are we talking?"

"Depends. What exactly do you want?" Hookers always like the john to specify a sex act before they talk price. That way, if it's a cop, they can claim entrapment.

"How about a half and half?"

She hesitated. Maggie might not be too smart, but she had good street sense. She could feel something wasn't quite right.

"How do I know you're not a cop?" she asked.

"I don't know. How does anyone know?"

"Pull it out," she said, gesturing toward my crotch.

"What?"

"Pull it out. Cops can't expose themselves."

I looked over at the people walking along the sidewalk a few feet away.

"What, right here?"

Maggie leaned into the car. "What's the matter? You shy?"

I shrugged, unzipped my fly, and did what she asked.

"Okay," she said. "Fifty bucks. Put it back before it catches cold." She opened the door and slid into the seat beside me. "Take a right at Seventeenth South."

120

She sniffed a couple of times, a good sign. She hadn't fixed yet.

"Let's get something to eat first," I said. She didn't look too thrilled with that idea, so I pulled out two twenties and a ten and handed them to her.

"I don't like to rush," I told her. "Besides, you seem like a nice lady, you know?"

She put the bills in her purse and relaxed. Now that she had the money she didn't care what we did.

I pulled into Perkins' at Fifteenth and State. A lot of the hookers eat there, so I felt she'd be more at ease. She waved at a couple of girls at a back table when we walked in.

I ordered pancakes, usually a fairly safe bet. Maggie got a club sandwich. She didn't seem very hungry, but she probably didn't want to pass up a free meal. While we ate, I avoided anything personal, picking topics out of *People* magazine. She brought up Mike Tyson and Robin Givens. It was old news, but she seemed to have a thing about it. I asked what she thought and listened respectfully to her opinion. She thought Robin Givens was a whore.

"She's no better than me or the rest of the girls on the street," she said. "Just another bitch trying to get what she can. That's fine, but she don't have to put on airs like her shit don't stink."

The conversation led around to street life, and how it was getting harder to make a buck with all the fourteen- and fifteen-year-olds selling it cheap.

"I used to have a good trade with the businessmen, you know?" she said. "All they want now is the real young stuff." She looked up, challenging me. "How old do you think I am?"

I studied her face. She looked in her early thirties, maybe older.

"I don't know," I said. "Twenty-five, maybe?"

"Twenty-three. Too old for most of them. The ones that do want me are kinky as hell. Shit, everyone wants something." She looked sharply at me. "You're not one of those, are you? Because I don't do that stuff."

"Don't worry," I said. "I'm as straight as they come. But you're right about one thing. Everybody wants something." I reached in my wallet and pulled out the packets of black tar. I dropped them on the table, one by one. Maggie eyed them greedily.

"Hey, you shouldn't be flashing that shit."

I folded my hands over them. "I'm looking for someone," I said.

"Fuck," she said, starting to get up from the table. "You *are* a cop."

"Wait a minute," I said, grabbing her arm. "You want to walk out of here, fine, but not with my fifty bucks." She hesitated, and I took my hand off the dope. "I'm not a cop; cops don't hand out free samples, you know that."

She sat back down. The combination of money and dope was too good to pass up.

"Shit," she said. "I was beginning to think you were just a nice guy."

"I am a nice guy. It's about those two black kids who were killed."

"I knew it. I never should have opened my mouth."

"Maggie, those were nice kids."

"Hey, shit happens."

"You sound like Becker."

"Who the fuck is Becker?"

"The cop you talked to down at the station."

"That prick? Somebody ought to do something about him, you know?"

"Some day somebody will." I pushed the tar over toward her. "So where is this guy, Maggie, the one who hates blacks?"

"I don't know. I already told the cops that. Why would I lie? I didn't have to say nothin'. And there's a reward, remember?"

"Sure," I said. "But maybe you started thinking what

122

would happen if this guy found out you turned him. Becker's not somebody you can trust, anyway, am I right?"

"He's a prick," she repeated.

"Come on, Maggie. You're not just another hooker. You're a nice lady. The guy drove around and talked to you. I'll bet he wanted to see you again, even."

The flattery seemed to get to her. "Yeah, he liked me," she admitted.

"And he didn't tell you where he's staying?" I unfolded my hands. Maggie looked at the dope longingly.

"No," she finally sighed. "He didn't."

I didn't move. "You sure?"

She nodded. It looked like I'd struck out this time.

"Oh, well," I said. I pushed the little packets over to her. "Here. Keep 'em." I got up and grabbed the check off the table. "Can I drop you somewhere?"

She swept the dope into her purse. "No, that's okay," she said. "I'll walk."

She followed me to the cashier and waited while I paid. On the way out the door she grabbed me by the arm.

"You know, I been thinking. Maybe there is something that might help you find him." I waited. "If you do, I'm out of it, right?" I nodded. "And I get some of the money?"

I nodded again. "If he's the right guy."

She licked her lips. "Well, he asked me where he could find a bar that was for whites only. I told him I didn't know any, but he could try the Bit and Spur. There aren't a whole lot of colored people that go there, you know?"

I knew. The Bit and Spur was redneck city.

"So, you might hang around there, I don't know."

"What does this guy look like?"

"Thirty, maybe thirty-five. Kind of heavy, dark hair. Like I told the cops, you can't miss him. He's got this scar right here." She put her finger up to the side of her face, right next to her left eye.

I nodded. "Thanks."

"Hey," she yelled as I got into my car, "don't forget about the money."

THE BIT AND SPUR IS A SEEDY BAR ON Eighth West without a whole lot to recommend it. I drove by and checked the cars out front for a Camaro with out of state plates. There were only two cars parked nearby, a Ford pickup and a Chevy Nova. It was still a little early for the bar scene.

I went in and used the phone, scoping out the place. It was really just one big room, with the omnipresent pool table in the back. There were four customers, and none of them paid me much attention.

I parked across the street and down the block where I had a good view of the entrance. A couple of hours passed before business started picking up, and another hour before a Camaro with Oklahoma plates showed up and parked in front. A heavyset man got out, locked the car carefully, and went into the bar.

I waited ten minutes and followed him inside. He was seated at the far end of the bar, against the wall, drinking a beer. I walked past him to the bathroom and got a good look at his face. The scar Maggie had described was there. When I came back out of the bathroom I sat down at the other end of the bar and ordered a draft. Now that I had him, I wasn't sure just where to take it. If he was anything like he'd made himself out to be, he wouldn't be cozying up for no reason to a stranger in a bar. On the other hand, he obviously liked to brag, or he wouldn't have played those games with Maggie. Maybe I could play on his weird trip about blacks.

I went to the phone on the wall and dialed Reggie's number. It rang eight times and I was about to hang up when he answered.

"Reggie," I said, "Jason. Don't talk, just listen. I might have a lead on those killings, and I need your help."

I explained what I wanted him to do. Reggie liked it but he had a few questions. I answered as best I could, went back to the bar, and waited for him to show up.

About twenty minutes later Reggie walked in, looked around, and took a seat on the stool next to me. I looked him over ostentatiously and moved down one seat. Reggie ignored me and ordered a beer, throwing a five on the bar. The bartender regarded him sourly but didn't say anything. When the change came back, Reggie scooped it up and looked at it incredulously.

"Just a minute, my man," he said. "I gave you a ten."

The bartender leaned across the bar and stuck his face out belligerently.

"First, I'm not 'your man,' second, you gave me a five."

I swiveled around on my stool and put my two cents in. "What kind of shit are you trying to pull, boy? I saw it; that was a five."

Reggie looked at me with a sneer. "Hey, cracker, why don't you stay out of things that ain't none of your business?"

"How about if I make it my business?" I said, standing up. The dialogue was a bit hokey, but the audience wasn't composed of drama critics.

Reggie got off his stool and stood facing me. This was the part he hadn't been so sure about. "Don't worry," I had told him. "Just throw the right hand directly toward the center of my face. If I know it's coming, it's easy. You won't hurt me."

"It's not you I'm worried about," he'd said. "It's that if I break my hand I won't be able to play for a month."

We stood facing each other, and Reggie balled up his fist. I was facing away from my audience at the end of the bar, so I nodded just perceptibly. Reggie threw the right and I moved left, guiding his arm past me and holding on to the wrist. He fell forward off balance and I continued through with the motion, ending up with his arm behind his back. I shifted to a come-along hold, put him up on his toes, and marched him out of the bar. I released him with a shove hard enough to put him on the ground.

"Hey, take it easy, Jase," he complained.

"Got to make it look good."

"So, how'd I do?"

"Perfect, you're a natural. Listen. Wait about half an hour and phone the police department. Ask for Dave Warren; he'll be on his pager. If they can't get through to him, anyone in Homicide. Tell them the man who was with Maggie May is at the Bit and Spur."

"Half hour, Dave Warren, Maggie May. Got it. Anything else?"

"That's it. See you later."

I turned on my heel and swaggered back into the bar. I sat down and ordered up another beer.

"Can you believe that spook?" I said, turning to the end of the bar where my target sat. "Fuckin' niggers think they own the world."

The man looked down the bar at me. "Where'd you learn that stuff?"

"Back in Nam. I learned a lot there. For one thing, I learned what happens when you let niggers mix in with white folks."

He picked up his beer and moved down the bar, taking the seat next to me.

"You from around here?" he asked.

I shook my head. "You?"

"Hell, no. This town sucks, you know?"

I agreed. We introduced ourselves. He told me his name was Eddie. We swapped racist jokes. My years on the police department had unfortunately provided me with a large supply. Reggie had given me a few more. We talked about how the country was going to the dogs, how a white man couldn't get a fair shake these days. He took a quick detour

126

onto the Jews, but I steered him back. When I felt I'd established my bona fides, I brought it up.

"Did you hear about those two niggers that were killed in the park?" I asked.

"Yeah," he said. "Fuckin' shame, wasn't it?" He laughed.

"They were with two white girls," I said. "I can't understand it. Why a white girl would mess around with a nigger. I just don't understand it."

"Well, they won't be messin' around with those particular niggers anymore, will they?" We both laughed.

I took a long swallow of beer, and looked around the bar. I leaned close and lowered my voice.

"Hey, you want to know something?" I said. "Those two nigger kids?" I paused for effect. "I killed them. Both of them."

I leaned back and waited for his reaction. Of course, I wasn't expecting him to say, "Bullshit, I'm the one who did it," or anything like that. What I was looking for was a little more subtle—a flash of that contemptuous, superior expression of someone who knows for a fact that you're full of crap.

"Holy shit!" he said. "You serious?"

His mouth was hanging open and his eyes shone with a mixture of awe and disbelief. Eddie hadn't shown himself to be overly bright so far, and unless he possessed a deeply hidden talent, he wasn't acting.

"What, you think I'm bullshitting you?" I asked.

Before he could answer the outside door opened and Dave Warren walked in with Mike Volter. Two steps behind them were Tony and another guy I didn't recognize. Reggie's phone call must have interrupted an interdepartmental meeting.

"Gotta take a piss," I said, and retired to the back wall.

They didn't waste any time taking Eddie down. He was spread-eagled across the bar before he knew what was happening. Dave pulled what looked like a .38 from under his shirt. They hustled him out of the bar, and I returned to my seat. The rest of the customers looked at me suspiciously. The bartender cleared off Eddie's half-finished beer without changing expression.

"Nice little place you've got here," I said to him.

Dave and Tony came back in. Dave leaned against the stool next to me.

"Very nice work," he said. "How'd you get on to him so quick?"

"Just lucky."

"Sure. He open up at all?"

"Nothing that would help." I glanced over at Tony. "I'll tell you, though, I don't think this guy is good for it."

"No? Why not?"

"Just a feeling. Wrong reaction to things I said."

Volter stuck his face back through the door, ignoring me.

"Let's go," he said, jerking his head at Dave.

Dave straightened up. "Mike's really got a hard-on for you, Jase," he said. "Talk to you later."

Tony waited until Dave was out the door. "So, you don't think this is the guy?"

"You heard me."

"Well, tell you what, I don't either. You still interested in those phone numbers you gave me, then? The ones from Dodgson?"

"You bet," I said.

"Okay. One of them is garbage, not listed to anything. Another is Godfather's Pizza. Then we've got a bar called the Matador."

"I know it. South Salt Lake. A lot of dopers go there, but it's pretty mellow. Anything else?"

"Oh, just a little coincidence." Tony sounded smug.

"Yeah?"

"The last number. Would you believe the residence of one Leonard R. Paxton, respected physician and all-around dirtbag?"

"You're putting me on."

"So long, Butte. Hello, Southern California."

I couldn't believe it. I had just about written Paxton off, despite the orgy he'd been at. "How about the address on B Street?" I asked.

"Nothing on that yet." He looked toward the front door. "Listen, I got to run before they take off without me. You interested in checking out the Matador by yourself, or you want to wait until I can get free?"

"Oh, I might drop in for a quick one."

"Watch yourself," Tony said.

IT WAS PAST EIGHT BY THE TIME I GOT TO the Matador. There weren't a lot of people there when I walked in—a few at the bar, a couple of guys playing pool at the usual table in the back. I sat at the bar and ordered a draft again. The bartender was a young guy who seemed disinclined to talk.

After a few minutes he came out from behind the bar and turned on a large screen TV sitting in one corner of the room. I was in luck. The Jazz were playing an exhibition game in Portland. You can't simply walk into a strange bar and start asking questions, not if you want answers. But there's nothing like a basketball game to transform a total stranger into just another one of the guys.

By the time the pregame show was over, the bar was about half full. I watched quietly until Karl Malone slammed through one of his patented dunks, then made a comment to the neighbor on my left. After a while I joined in with the general banter. At halftime I had a spirited discussion about how the Jazz had blown the play-offs last year and whether the trade for Jeff Malone would really help. At the end of the third quarter I bought several people beers.

The Jazz won the game by two points, and by that time I was one of the gang. We all had another beer and did a postmortem on the game. Finally someone commented they hadn't seen me around before.

"Just got into town a few days ago," I said. "I come in and out. In fact, last time I was here I met a guy who told me this was a pretty mellow bar, so I thought I'd check the place out." I looked around. "You know, it's not bad, except nobody here knows shit about the finer points of basketball."

There was a lot of hooting over that statement and we went around with it for a while, mock serious.

"I was kind of hoping to see this guy here," I said after the noise died down. "Name's Roger, Roger Dodge, I think."

"Dodge?" said a guy I'd learned was Miles. "I don't think so. I'm here almost every night—"

"No shit," put in one of the others.

"I'm here almost every night," Miles repeated, ignoring him, pushing a pair of heavy-framed glasses back up his nose. "I can't remember anyone named Dodge being around. What's he look like?"

I was stuck for an answer, since I didn't know. I briefly considered describing Roger the last time I'd seen him, but I didn't think it would go over real big. I made up something nebulous and got blank looks.

After a while people started drifting home. Nobody seemed to have any interest in Roger or who he might be, and I didn't think they were kidding me. A wasted evening. All that time to gain their trust, and it turns out nobody had ever heard of him. Sometimes it goes that way.

I looked around for the phone and spotted it on the back wall past the pool table. I got up and headed toward it to call Laura and then realized it was a little late. I wandered back to the bar. I still had half a beer left, but didn't feel like hanging around. I took a final gulp and headed home.

The clouds pressed in as I reached the mouth of the canyon. White tendrils started creeping across the road, and by the time I was halfway up I was driving through fog so thick I couldn't see the shoulder. My headlights poked a narrow tunnel through the swirling whiteness as the mist wrapped itself around the car. I felt eerily cut off from the rest of the world. In fact, for all I knew, the world outside no longer existed. I dwelt on the idea for a while. There was just me and the wind and the fog and the hum of the engine changing pitch as the canyon steepened and leveled. It was a musical whine. I could almost recognize the tune. I listened carefully, trying to catch it. Was I traveling five miles an hour or fifty? Hard to say. The fog created complex patterns outside my windshield, gray and white and blue, changing and shifting in a swirling vortex.

The car bounced and shuddered, and I realized with panic I was on the shoulder heading off the road. I hit the brakes and slid to a stop just on the edge. The headlight beams angled up and cut into the fog like two World War II searchlights seeking out enemy planes.

The engine had died, and I sat in the stillness listening to my hoarse breathing. In, out, in, out. I took a huge breath. My mind wasn't working too well, but well enough to realize something was terribly wrong.

I looked down at the hand grasping the steering wheel. My arm stretched out away from me, miles long. The hand seemed to be more part of the steering wheel than part of the arm. I wondered how I could detach it. I closed my eyes, but it didn't help. The inside of my head became its own little universe, and I forgot there was a world outside. When I inadvertently opened my eyes again and saw the inside of the car, I felt a huge disorienting wrench.

I'd been dosed. It wasn't LSD; I'd tried that a couple of times back in the seventies. There were some similarities, but it wasn't acid. One part of my mind was drifting, but there was another part unaffected, cool and analytical, watching the whole thing. PCP, I thought. That was the most likely. Distortions of body image. Auditory and visual confusion. Yep, I thought with satisfaction, clinically ticking off the symptoms. PCP. Someone in the bar. They hadn't heard of Roger. Good old Roger Dodger. Sure they hadn't.

What I had to do was get home. I'd be safe there. I managed to get the car started and pulled back on the road. The clinical side of my mind knew I was crazy. It wondered dispassionately if I'd make it home or if I'd drive right off the edge. It knew I should pull over and wait it out. But I couldn't. I had to get home. Home was safe.

I tried hard to focus on the road. The fog ahead started glowing red. Two eyes were staring at me, growing larger and brighter, huge tiger eyes. The tiger. The tiger remembered.

I almost drove right up into the rear of the car in front of me before the eyes resolved themselves into taillights. A VW was creeping along in the fog. I wondered how fast I had been going to run up on it like that.

I settled down behind it and followed those lights. It would be my guide. Jennifer had owned a VW. She would be my guide. She would take me home. Roger had had a VW too, though. I strained through the fog. I could see him, one leathered hand wrapped around the wheel, ruined face turned back over one shoulder, urging me on with a ghastly smile.

The part of my mind that watched took me in hand. It's the drug, it said. That's just a car. There is no Roger. There is no Jennifer. It's a car. Follow it. Keep your distance and follow it.

It wasn't until we passed Snowbird and the VW turned off that the fog cleared. It was still thick in patches, but now at least I could see the road. The black asphalt panted and shimmied. I made it the rest of the way to the cabin, somehow pulled myself out of the car, and slowly climbed the mountain of stairs that led to the front door.

Stony hopped down from the couch when I came in. He looked up at me, stretched, and yawned. His teeth gleamed white against the redness inside his mouth, and I could see saliva dripping off them. He gaped wide enough to swallow me whole. I took a step backward and got hold of myself again. Just a cat, Jase. Just a cat.

I put my mind on autopilot, trying to settle down with familiar tasks. I opened a can of cat food, ignoring the fact that it squirmed when I put it on the plate. I washed a few dishes. I thought about music but decided not. Finally I sat down in the chair by the window and stared outside. The fog hadn't reached up this high, and the moon poured down on the mountaintops, still dusted with snow, cold and inhuman. The lines coming off the telephone pole outside the window glowed and crackled, humming with vibrant colors, red to green to yellow.

After a couple of hours things started coming back into shape. I realized I was exhausted. I staggered downstairs to the bedroom, stopping to wash my face with some cold water. I glanced up and saw my face in the mirror. That was a mistake. The reflection glowed with a life of its own, a separate existence. I locked eyes with it, unable to turn away. It stared back at me with a knowing and crafty look. I know you, it said. You may fool all the others, but I know you. This is what you are. Look. Look.

The face changed, dissolving and melting, but it was always me. It wore a sly and cunning expression, unpleasant and smug and horribly familiar. The expression a warped child might have torturing a small animal.

It stared at me, leering and gloating. There was sickness there, but also power and strength and a compelling sexuality. Hyde is always more potent than Jekyll. Lust, and hate, and boastful triumph. The change went deeper, the face now scarcely human, but it was still me. Look, it said. This is what's under the skin. This is you. This is all of us. It was loathsome. It was cruel and brutal and ruthless. But most of all it was . . . ultimately selfish. Me, me, me, that's all that counts, it said. That's all that really matters. It was the face beyond reason, the animal lust in the dark that perpetuates the species, the mindless grasping of the drowning man who climbs over his best friend to reach up for the light and the sweet air. Me. Me. Me.

I wrenched away my gaze, sick to my heart. I staggered into the bedroom and threw myself face down on the bed, letting unconsciousness overtake me. All that night I dreamed, bizarre images and formless terrors. And always, over and over, something else I could never quite see.

10

I slept fourteen hours, if you could call it sleep. More like a drugged stupor. Sometime during the night I'd managed to get the blankets around me and was in a fetal position with them wrapped around me. I sat up and reached for a cigarette. Not a good thing—I could remember not so long ago when I never lit one until I'd had my first cup of coffee.

Stony was curled up at the foot of the bed and he sat up when I did, yawning and stretching. He padded over and plopped down in the crook of my arm. I grabbed his paw gently and he purred. It was still swollen, but looked pretty good.

I finally pulled myself out of bed, started some coffee, gave Stony a belated breakfast, and took a long shower. By the time I was dressed and drinking coffee it was four in the afternoon. The fog had turned into snow sometime during the night, then back into rain, and there was a white glaze covering the trees. Stony hopped up on the bookcase by the window and stared out dejectedly, ears flat. I stared out with the same emotion, wondering if my car would make it out.

The message machine had one call from Dave and three from Tony. He sounded worried. The FBI office would be closed by now, but I called the informant number and left a message.

I made another pot of coffee and began to feel more human. The PCP hadn't seemed to leave too much of an aftereffect, although the edges of things still wavered a bit. I'd been lucky. Lucky not to have run right off the canyon road, and luckier still I hadn't gotten more of a dose. Someone at the Matador hadn't cared much for my questions about Roger. It must have been when I left my beer to use the telephone. When I'd come back, I'd taken just a final swallow. If I'd finished that beer, I'd have swallowed ten times the dose. Considering what the little I'd drunk had done to me, I didn't even want to think about what a megadose would have been like.

About five Tony called again.

"Jason!" he said, sounding relieved. "Where the hell have you been? I was getting worried."

"Just sleeping."

"What, all day?"

"I had a strenuous night." I told him what had happened.

"Son of a bitch! I should have gone with you. Any idea who it was?"

"Sure. Any one of about thirty people."

"Jesus. You okay? Should you see a doctor?"

"I'm fine."

"You sure?"

"Yeah, I'm fine. What's up?"

"Well, you know that girl, Debbie, who's in the hospital?"

"Yeah?"

"I went to see her this morning. Only, she isn't there anymore."

"They release her?"

"More like she just walked out."

"I wanted to talk to her again."

"You and me both. Any idea where she might have gone?"

"Not really, unless she just went home, which isn't likely. I could run out there and check, though."

"You sure you want to go alone? You didn't do so well by yourself last time, remember. It could be trouble."

"I don't think so. They're not dangerous, and these particular people aren't going to be too fond of the FBI ever since the Singer fiasco."

"Oh. Polygamists?"

"Exactly. I'll let you know what I come up with."

"Let me give you another number," he said. "I'll probably be in another meeting."

I drank another quick cup of coffee, put on a heavy shirt, brushed the snow off my car, and headed down the road. The car slipped and slid, but the front-wheel drive helped. I made it without too much trouble down to where the snow-plows end, right past the Snowpine Lodge. Going up would be a different matter.

I drove down the canyon and out toward Riverton, the same direction Tony and I had taken a couple of days earlier. It took me a while to locate the place. I finally found it at the end of a dirt lane. Along the lane were apple orchards, and brown fields stretched out all around. The house was two storied, long and narrow, covered in brown shingles and a peaked roof. There was a door in the middle and doors at either end. Six or seven young kids were playing on a tire swing hanging from a tree in the front yard, and as soon as I pulled up they all scooted into the house. A minute later a blond kid, maybe seventeen, came out. He was wearing overalls. He greeted me as I stepped out of my car.

"Good afternoon," he said, very formal. "Can I help you, sir?"

I groped for a moment for Debbie's brother's name. "I'd like to talk to Levi. Levi Shaw?"

"Levi?" He thought for a moment. "I think he's out back. I'll try to find him for you." He paused, struggling to decide whether it was proper to invite me in or not. Finally hospitality won out over discretion.

"Would you like to wait inside?" he asked.

I followed him into the house. The front room was spotless, a large parlor with a couple of couches and a baby grand in the corner. A staircase led to the top floor and a long corridor ran the length of the house. There were two more staircases at either end. The floors were polished wood and the walls were bare.

I sat down on one of the couches and the young man left me alone. About two minutes had passed when I heard a step on the top of the middle stairway. A young girl started down the stairs, then stopped when she saw me. Her hair was pinned up and she wore a floor-length dress that was almost a robe. She stared at me curiously.

"I'm waiting to see Levi," I said.

She came down the rest of the stairs and sat suddenly on the bottom step.

"You're looking for Debbie, aren't you?" she said. She had a thin whispery voice, a lot like Debbie's.

"Is she here?"

The girl didn't answer. "You're a cop, aren't you?"

"You Debbie's sister?"

She smiled, showing beautiful teeth. "She's a year older. I'm Verily."

"I'm Jason," I said, "and I'm not a cop. That's a very pretty name, Verily."

"It's from the Bible, you know."

I digested that for a minute. "Are you two close?"

"Me and Debbie? We used to be. Then she got into this weird stuff. You know about that?"

"Yeah," I said. "I'm afraid I do."

She nibbled on her thumb. "Are you religious?" she asked suddenly.

I considered. "No, I can't really say as I am."

She smiled again. "Oh, good. I'm not either." Silence again, while she looked me over.

"Is Debbie okay?" she asked.

"I don't know. I hope so. I'd like to find her."

Verily levered herself up a couple of steps. "I don't know where she is."

"You know, next time they might kill her," I said quietly.

She pondered that for a few seconds. "I don't trust cops," she said.

I flashed her a smile. "I can't say as I blame you. I don't trust them a whole lot myself."

We sat in silence for a while longer, then she suddenly made up her mind. Maybe it was my remark about cops. Maybe she was worried about Debbie herself.

"Okay. Just be cool, huh? Most of the time she stays with a girl called Melody. I don't know where she lives. She has an apartment somewhere. But there's another place Debbie likes to crash. You know where Fairmont Park is?" I nodded. "Okay, well, right past where the softball field is, you know where the freeway is?" I nodded again. "There's a street right after the freeway overpass, and if you go down it there's a little dead end street in the middle. Right there is a spooky old abandoned house. Debbie used to stay there when she needed a place to crash."

Before I could ask anything else, the young blond kid in overalls came back in the room. He stared at Verily until she scrambled to her feet and ran back up the stairs.

"I'm sorry," he said. "I thought Levi was here, but he's not. He'll be back later."

"Sorry I missed him," I said, "but that's okay. I'll get hold of him some other time."

The boy followed me back out to my car and watched as

I drove away. Verily had given me more than I had hoped for. This time, I decided not to go it alone. I called Tony from a Circle K, interrupting his meeting, and told him what I'd found out.

"Can you meet me at the Fairmont parking lot by the ball field?" I asked. "We can head over there together."

"Give me an hour," he said.

I followed Verily's directions to make sure the house was where she said it was and then waited in the Fairmont lot for Tony. He was late, and it was getting dark by the time he drove up. My car was facing out, and he pulled in next to me so the driver's-side windows were about six inches apart. It's the standard way patrol cops talk to each other in every city. Since you're facing in opposite directions, it's hard for anyone to come up on you.

"Sorry," he said through the window. "I had to sit in on another task force meeting and listen to more bullshit theories about crazed racists."

"What about the guy in the Bit and Spur? Anything come of that?"

Tony laughed. "You're not gonna believe this. The guy's a salesman, on the western circuit. And you know what Mr. Macho sells? Get this. Underwear. Men's underwear."

"Did he talk?"

"Talk? I'll say he talked. He squealed like a piglet. But what he wanted to talk about was you. He was so eager to turn you we could hardly shut him up."

I laughed. "You know, I'm a little disappointed. I thought we white folks stuck together."

"Sure. Hey, that sergeant, Volter, was sure pissed. Wanted to do you on interference with an investigation, but your friend Dave Warren talked him out of it. Anyway, they're holding the guy on a weapons charge for the thirty-eight he was packing, hoping they can come up with something on him."

Tony leaned back in his seat and lit a cigarette. "What do you think that guy's up to?" he asked casually.

That's another thing cops do, if they have any respect for who they're with. They don't ask, "Do you see that guy?" They assume you see whatever they see. In this case Tony was talking about a character across the street I'd been watching myself. Tony had caught him in his rearview mirror. The guy was walking slowly along the street, peering into the parked cars.

"Just some fuck about to do a car prowl," I said.

"Well, shit, let's get out of here before we have to do something about it. You know where this house is?"

"Follow me," I said, and started up my car.

THE STREET WAS RIGHT OFF THE MIDDLE of Parkway Avenue. We parked on the corner and walked the rest of the way in. When we got to the end of the block I pointed.

"There it is."

It was a creepy-looking two-story house, the kind that neighborhood kids would go to on Halloween. The boys would tell their girlfriends about horrible murders that took place there. The girls wouldn't believe a word, but they wouldn't go in anyway. Directly across the street there were other houses, but on either side of the house were empty lots.

The windows were boarded up, and in the dusk I could see weathered paint hanging in strips from the walls. The front door was just a gaping hole. Behind the house, open space stretched up to the freeway that ran along the rear.

"Great atmosphere," Tony muttered.

"Let's take a look," I said.

We stood by the front-door opening for a couple of minutes, listening. Nothing. Tony nodded at me and I slipped inside. A bare room greeted me. A shaky-looking set of stairs led up to the second floor and another stairway, probably to the basement, stretched down into darkness from an open doorway.

Tony came up beside me and whispered in my ear. "I'll check upstairs, you see what's down below."

He moved off before I could say anything. I didn't like it. It was too much like those grade-B horror movies where there's someone or something on the loose, and everyone splits up. "You take the attic, I'll check the basement; Marsha, you check out the empty greenhouse." The audience knows that at least one of the cast is going to end up horribly dismembered.

I shrugged and started making my way down the basement steps. They seemed solid; they didn't even squeak. I pointed my flashlight down and saw that someone had replaced several of the steps with new planks. The house wasn't quite as abandoned as it seemed. Halfway down, in the corner by the wall, lay an empty pill bottle. Codeine phosphate, one hundred tablets, not a regular prescription vial, a pharmacy stock bottle. There was a printed code and some numbers written on a sticker on the side. I slipped it in my pocket and made my way down the rest of the steps.

The basement was dank and moldy. A row of narrow windows, just aboveground, sat at eye level. They were loosely boarded up, but the last of the afternoon light filtered through the cracks. A ratty mattress lay in one corner, covered by a filthy blanket. I flashed my light around the room. Toward the back was a long, narrow table. On the wall behind the table, scrawled in large letters with something that looked suspiciously like blood, were the words NIGGER LOVER.

There was something lying under that table I couldn't quite make out. I didn't know if I really wanted to. Part of it was sticking out, a part that might possibly be a bare foot. I got a bad feeling. I got a very bad feeling. I walked over to the table, focused my flashlight, and knelt down.

A woman was lying under the table, on her back, right leg straight, left leg crooked to the side, an obscene parody of invitation. There was a bandage on the leg. A long flannel shirt had been pulled up to just under her neck and then thrown over her head. I couldn't see her face, but I could see that her throat had been cut. She was naked underneath the shirt. A toothbrush, bristles upright, projected grotesquely out of her vagina. A spill of long colorless hair flowed out from under the shirt. There was a lot of blood pooled around the area of her head and neck, fresh blood, barely starting to congeal around the edges. In the middle of her chest, a knife projected, standing straight. It was a Ginsu knife, the kind they advertise on TV. It chops, it slices, it dices, I thought grimly. It had been driven into her with such force that it looked like it had gone right through her body and was sticking into the ground beneath her.

I didn't really need to, but I reached down and carefully pulled the shirt back from her face. Maybe it wasn't her. It was. Debbie Shaw stared back at me with blank eyes.

11

All those years as a street cop are what saved me. When I heard the footstep behind me and the whooshing sound I threw myself sideways and the club glanced off my shoulder, numbing my arm. My flashlight went flying into the corner and went out. I kept rolling, reaching across my body with my left arm, trying to get my Walther out of my belt. My right arm wasn't going to be much use for a while.

I could just make out a figure coming after me. It raised its arm and I caught a silvery glint. Aluminum bat, I thought with that total detachment you sometimes get in a life and death situation. Not legal in the major leagues. I rolled back the other way and just made it under the table as the bat came down, splintering the tabletop. I hunched up against Debbie's body, still scrabbling for my gun with my left hand. I finally managed to get it free and fired three rounds blindly up through the tabletop. The dim figure immediately threw the bat under the table at me. It glanced off my knee and he sprinted toward the stairs. I scrambled out from under the table and stumbled over something in the darkness, going down again. As I got to my feet, limping, there was a yell from the top of the stairs, then a crash of someone going down hard, then a loud "Motherfuck!" I staggered up the stairs just in time to catch Tony climbing to his feet, shaking his head, trying to clear it. His gun was on the floor five feet away.

I ran over to the front door and looked out. The street was empty, but there were curtains moving in the front window of the house across the street.

"I heard shots," Tony said, coming up next to me, breathing hard. He glanced up and down the empty street. "Where the fuck did he go? I came flying down the stairs, and ran right into some guy coming up through the basement doorway. You all right?"

"Sort of. You get a look at him?"

He shook his head. "Too dark. What happened, Jase?"

"Whoever it was came at me with a baseball bat. I got off a couple of rounds but I don't think I hit him."

Tony nodded thoughtfully. "Take you out, wait till I come down wondering what you're up to, and take me out. Pretty slick."

The feeling was coming back into my right arm as he spoke, and the shoulder was starting to hurt like hell. I moved it cautiously.

"Shoulder?" Tony asked.

"Yeah. Nothing broken, I think."

"Let's get it looked at. And let's get out of here before somebody official shows up."

"Take a look in the basement first."

He started to ask a question, then slipped down the stairs, leaving me standing in the dark. In a minute he was back again.

"We're getting out of here, Jase, fast."

"We can't do that."

"Fuck we can't." He pointed out the open doorway at the house across the street where a face was now peering cautiously from the front window.

"The cops will be here any minute. There's nothing we can do, and when the bureau finds me here with you I'm going to be in deep shit."

I hesitated. Tony pulled at my good arm, and for the first time since I'd met him, he totally lost his cool. I could hear the beginnings of panic in his voice.

"Come *on*, Jase, let's book!"

I gave in; I wasn't all that eager to stay around anyway. We made it back down the street to our cars without running into anyone. By now I had enough use of my arm back to use the gearshift and I slid carefully behind the wheel. Tony wanted to go somewhere and talk things over. He was beside himself with the idea that we'd had the guy and missed him. I begged off.

"Tomorrow," I said.

My mind was numb, and I didn't want to get into it right now. I could see Tony wasn't happy, but he didn't want to stand in the street arguing, not with the cops about to show up any second. He gave me a quick nod.

"Tomorrow, then. Do me a favor and try not to get yourself killed before then, will you, Jase?"

"I'll certainly do my best," I said, gingerly putting the car in gear. Two blocks down Ninth East a black and white passed, traveling fast. As it turned the corner the headlights went off.

I was a lot more shaken than I'd wanted to admit—not just physically; my psyche was bruised as well. I thought of the cold drive up the canyon to an empty house and decided I didn't feel like being alone just yet. I stopped at a 7-Eleven and dialed Laura's number. She answered on the third ring. The welcoming tone in her voice was a lift.

"I was wondering if you'd call," she said.

"How could you doubt it?"

"One never knows. Are you coming by?"

"I thought I might."

"Well, good. I don't have to get up tomorrow."

*　　*　　*

WHEN SHE OPENED HER DOOR IT SUR-prised me just how good it felt to see her. She was wearing a patterned robe that swirled when she moved. Her hair was loose and just washed. She gave me a quick hug and I could smell its damp freshness. She steered me into the kitchen.

"Tea's ready," she said.

It was strong and black and reassuring. Coffee was something that kept me going. Tea was a respite. I could see how people got into it.

Laura sat down across from me, the sleeves of her robe falling over her hands. She pushed them back and started toying with a long strand of hair. I eased into the chair across from her.

"You okay?" she asked, noticing the way I moved.

"Just a bit bruised. I ran into a little trouble tonight."

"Oh?"

I hesitated. I felt an overwhelming compulsion to tell her about it, every graphic detail, as if that would somehow exorcise the blood-soaked image of Debbie from my brain. I got myself under control.

"We found another body" was all I finally said. It didn't seem to faze her.

"Was it bad?"

"Yeah. Pretty bad."

"How did you get hurt?"

I told her, trying to pass it off lightly. She was suitably impressed.

"Let me make sure I've got this straight. There are all these people getting killed and you go into an empty house and wander down into a dark basement by yourself?"

"It doesn't sound real bright, does it?"

"Do you have any idea who it was?"

"Right now I don't have any idea about anything." I

thought for a moment and then laughed, a little hysterically.

Laura looked at me with concern. "What is it?"

"You want to know how I feel? Did you ever read Scrooge McDuck comics when you were a kid?"

"Sure," she said, humoring me.

"Well, there was this one story called 'The Lemming with the Locket.' Carl Barks did it; he was a genius. Scrooge puts the only combination to his money bin in a locket, trying to simplify his life. Somehow, the locket gets caught around a lemming, which escapes. He chases the lemming all the way to Norway, where it joins with a huge tide of the little critters heading toward the sea. Out of that whole sea of rodents, Scrooge has to find that one particular lemming. There's this one panel where lemmings are swarming all over him, through his legs, past his ears, just thousands of them. All he can say is, 'Oh me, how did I ever get into this?'"

"Oh, come on. It's not that bad, is it?"

"Close. I don't have a clue. Everywhere I go dead people are turning up, and I still don't have the faintest idea what's going on."

She got up and came around in back of my chair, putting her hands lightly on my shoulders. "This hurt?"

I shook my head. She rubbed my shoulders gently, barely touching, and bent down over me. Her hair spilled over my shoulder into my face.

"We could visit my loft if it would help any."

I put my hands over hers. The image of Debbie was fresh in my mind. I didn't think I wanted to do anything. I didn't think I *could* do anything. I tilted my head up toward hers to explain, saw her smiling at me, and a wave of desire rolled through my body. It wasn't lust, not exactly. It didn't have anything to do with love. It was sheer need. I couldn't even speak. I just got to my feet and held her close, burying my face in her hair.

Sex and death, that's what this whole case was about. Sex is exuberant, alive, the most vital thing we do. Or should be. That's what made Debbie so disturbing and grotesque. Not just her death, but the hideous sexual implication. That twisted reversal, the total negation of all that's good and sweet in life. The intertwining of death and sex. The true Black Art. And in front of me, Laura. Vibrant, lusty, sexual, totally alive.

In a minute I'd recovered enough to follow her up the slanted ladder that led to her loft. Most of the space was filled by a large bed covered with a dark spread of intricate pattern.

"One of yours?"

"Of course. It took so long to make I couldn't afford to sell it."

Next to the bed was a low bureau. A large photo of a young man on a windsurfer sat on top. He had shoulder-length blond hair and a surfer tan. Laura saw me looking at it.

"My semi-ex-husband," she explained.

"Okay," I said after a minute. "I'll bite. What's a semi-ex-husband?"

"A husband you've divorced but can't quite seem to get out of your life."

"Your choice or his?"

"A little of both." She reached over and laid the picture flat on the bureau. "I hate it when he watches."

We sat down on the edge of the bed and she put her arms around my neck. We kissed for a while and slowly toppled over. We kissed a while longer, and my hand strayed to the belt of her robe.

"No fair," she said. "You still have your clothes on."

I remedied that, undid the belt, and pulled her robe open. Below her stomach she was blond and thick and luxuriant. I ran my hand down her body. She was soft, but firm where it counted. I was getting firm myself.

She rolled over on top of me, her robe covering both of

us. She shifted her legs slightly and I entered her, very slowly, no preliminaries. She sighed and began rocking back and forth, very easy. It felt so good I wanted to cry. After a while we rolled back over and continued. Then we did some other things. Then we did some more other things. Then I lost myself for a while in that eternal rhythm of flesh against flesh, life calling to life. After a long time, when we both were done, she hugged me tightly to her.

"Umm," she said. "Very, very nice indeed."

"That it was."

Laura would never know how much those simple words really meant. I lay there a minute, spent, then propped myself up on an elbow and reached for a cigarette.

"I suppose this is a nonsmoking loft?" I said, hesitating.

"Usually. I make exceptions." She stretched up to the bureau and handed me a ceramic dish. "Here. Use this."

I sat up and lit a cigarette, watching the smoke curl off into the shadows in the corner of the loft.

"You're thinking again, aren't you?" Laura said.

"Sorry."

"That's okay." She brushed my shoulder lightly. It was turning interesting colors.

"Ouch," she said. "I didn't realize. Maybe we shouldn't have done anything."

"More than worth it. Now I can die happy."

We were both quiet for a while, and then she said, "Why do people do such awful things?"

"What things?"

"You know. Murder. All that sick stuff."

"That's what I've been trying to figure. Usually it's simple. Somebody gets mad, usually over something stupid. Or they get scared and strike out at someone. But this is different, just way out there. I don't think it's a racist. I don't think it's just a crazy. And I don't really think it's got anything to do with any occult plot." I sighed. "The trouble is, I don't know what I think."

"Maybe you're making it all too complicated. How long were you a cop?"

"Long enough."

"Then you've seen a lot of things. So why do people kill each other? If it isn't just anger, I mean, or fear."

"Two things mostly." I answered automatically, without thinking. "Sex or money."

I stared at the ceiling. Sex or money. What had Laura said the other night about the Triangle people? Not really occult. A sex thing. Little Monica apparently had quite a propensity for sexual blackmail. The pictures of Monica I'd found in Roger's basement were numbered, one through ten, two of them missing. Sex *and* money. Monica was only sixteen, a scary thought for whoever was in those photos. Sex and money. Whose face was hidden in those pictures?

Roger Dodger had kept some of those prints. Roger was dead in his VW. Monica was in those photos. She was missing, possibly dead herself by now. Isaac was Monica's boyfriend. Isaac was dead, gunned down in the park. Debbie was in their group. Debbie was dead. A very tight little group. So, maybe no crazed racists, no ritual murders, no occult plots. Just a simple equation. Sex plus money equals death. But it was an awful lot of death just to keep a face hidden.

So, somebody important had to be involved. Doc Paxton? No way. If nothing else, he was too chubby. Not him in the photos. He'd never be able to carry it off, anyway. Some friend or colleague of his, someone high in the Mormon church? Possible, I guess. A politician, someone with friends, someone whose career would be ruined by a sex scandal? A lawyer? A judge? Maybe even a . . .

"Oh, my God," I said.

"What's wrong?"

A sick feeling spread through my stomach. "Everything." I looked up at the beams in the ceiling. "Stupid, stupid. Unbelievably stupid."

"What?"

"Me. Oh, Jesus."

"You're not making much sense, Jason."

"I just had a thought," I said. "Not a good thought. In fact, a very bad thought."

She looked at me doubtfully and I reached over with my good arm to pull her closer. She snuggled up close to me.

"Are you going to spend the night?" she asked after a while. I stroked her hair.

"I can't," I said.

I thought she'd take it as an affront, but she surprised me. "That's okay," she said. "To tell the truth, I'm not real comfortable myself spending the night with someone I don't know too well."

"You didn't seem all that uncomfortable a while ago."

"Sex is easy. Waking up with someone the next morning is a little more personal."

I silently smoked my cigarette. When it was finished I stubbed it out carefully and reached for my clothes. Laura slipped on her robe and we clambered down the ladder. At the door, she gave me a good night kiss on the cheek, very chaste.

"See you soon, I hope?"

"Soon," I said. "And often."

I KNEW I WAS RIGHT; THERE COULDN'T BE any other answer. I still wanted confirmation, though. Doubts were already beginning to creep in. I took a short drive up to the Avenues. As I turned off South Temple it started to rain.

271 B Street looked as deserted as it had the day I drove by with Melvin on the way to the hospital. I parked around the corner, took my bag out from under the spare tire, walked to the house, and without hesitation strolled down the driveway and around to the back.

Six-foot hedges ringed the backyard, providing privacy from prying neighbors. Also providing privacy for aspiring burglars. Three steps led up to a small stoop by the back door. The door was a strong solid-core oak secured with a good deadbolt lock, but like so many places, that's where the security stopped. Three small rectangular panes of opaque glass ran diagonally across the top half.

I had some relatively sophisticated stuff in my burglar bag but I wouldn't need it. I took out the roll of duct tape and covered the pane nearest the doorknob with a couple of layers. I slipped on my gloves and rapped sharply on the taped pane with the heel of my hand. Nothing happened, except my hand hurt. I took the pry bar out of the bag and tried again, with a bit more success. There was a muffled crunching sound, nothing that could be heard on the street. I knocked about half the pane out, just enough to get my arm in, reached through down to the knob, and unlocked the door.

I stepped into a large kitchen and closed the door behind me. I listened for a moment. I could hear the ticking of a clock in the living room and the sound of the rain splashing against the windows. Nothing else.

I flashed my light quickly around the kitchen. It was clean and bare. I walked through into the living room and, like any good burglar, immediately unlocked the front door. It's always good to have more than one direction to go if you have to get out in a hurry. I took a quick look through the living room. A couple of armchairs and a couch. A few books in the wall bookshelves. A carpeted staircase led to the upper story.

Upstairs was a bathroom and two small bedrooms with a double bed in each one. The first one had a night table and a small bureau. I opened the bureau drawers. There was an old bedspread in the bottom drawer and a couple of magazines in one of the top drawers. Nothing else. The other bedroom was pretty much the same, although there was a sweatshirt hanging in the closet. It was pretty clear this was a house no one lived in.

I checked the night table in the first bedroom, under the

beds, behind the bureaus. There had to be something, something that showed Monica had been here. And the other thing I wanted confirmation about. I went back to the other bedroom and shined my light up on the shelf in the top of the closet. There was a shoe box shoved back into the corner, and I hauled it down. Neatly stacked inside were a bunch of papers. Very sloppy procedure. What if a burglar broke in? I didn't bother to pull the papers out. I didn't need to. They weren't exactly what I was used to, but the form was familiar enough to be unmistakable. They were disbursement chits.

Every law enforcement office uses disbursement chits. If you pay money to an informant, if you buy dope, if you purchase stolen goods—the money you spend has to be accounted for. Chits are supposed to stay in the office, but everyone cuts corners to save a little time. Sometimes they're left at the safe house.

A safe house is a location to meet snitches, not a house to live in. That's why this place was so bare and sterile. Informants are paranoid; they aren't about to walk into a police station. They don't even want to be seen in public if they can help it, not with a cop. You can't hardly blame them.

So you need an out-of-the-way house or apartment where you can get together with them. The county sheriff's office has a safe house. The city has two. The addresses change every six months or so.

Other agencies use safe houses, too. I gazed down at the chits in the shoebox. On top of these particular vouchers was printed FEDERAL BUREAU OF INVESTIGATION.

12

When I got back up the canyon the rain had changed to snow again, this time, hard. I parked by the post office and surveyed the road leading up to the cabin. Too much snow to risk the car; if I drove up I'd never get out in the morning. Not quite enough snow on the ground yet to use the snowmobile. I sighed and started out on foot.

I wasn't dressed for snow, but the hike warmed me. Snowstorms have a special muffled stillness to them, and only the sound of my breathing and the crunch of the snow underneath my feet broke the quiet. Large flakes drifted in front of my eyes, invisible in the dark until they melted on my face.

Halfway to the cabin I stopped and listened to the wind pushing through the trees. I could smell the fresh snow and the trees and the cold air. A heavy depression settled over me. What the hell was I doing mixed up in all this? Dead bodies. Psycho killers. I had been racing around at top speed—conning twisted racists, frightening pathetic, sweaty doctors, talking up whores on the street. For what? None of it matters, said the trees. This is what's real: the wind and the snow and the trees. Of course, they said, there are many realities to choose from. You could choose this. But you choose the other. It's your choice.

I shook it off and started walking again. I didn't have time for philosophizing. One of these days I'd be standing lost in a daydream and someone would come along and blow the top of my head off. There's a reality for you.

The rhythm of my steps got me thinking. I couldn't believe how easily I'd been played. Doc Paxton, heavy into the occult, the connection with Monica, a logical suspect. Who put me on to him? Tony. Strengthen the case with Roger Dodger—Roger had Paxton's phone number—or so said Tony. More useful information. Who sent me to the Matador, where a helpful sort had done a small favor for a friend, no questions asked? Why, the ever helpful Tony, of course. I'd never even thought of checking what he told me. The only information I'd ever come up with on my own was where Debbie was hiding, and I handed that over to Tony immediately. Another brilliant move. No wonder he was late meeting me at Fairmont Park. He'd just had enough time to rush over and kill Debbie before he met me.

Not to mention that when there are two people in an otherwise empty house, and one of them almost gets his skull crushed, you might think an alert fellow like myself would have at least a glimmering as to who might have done it. But oh no, not me.

Some things still weren't clear. Tony had his sex trip going, passing himself off as "Narada"; that much was obvious. Thinking with his dick again. Then he met Monica, a tasty morsel if ever there was one. But with Monica, sex wasn't the main thing, just a means to an end. For her, sex and blackmail went together like bread and butter. The FBI is pretty straight arrow. They wouldn't take kindly to an agent screwing around with an underage girl. It would get him fired. It might even get him prosecuted. Of course, it was just her word against his. So she needed a little help.

Enter Roger Dodger. Enter the photo session. Exit Roger Dodger.

When Roger disappeared, courtesy of Special Agent Anthony Hill, Monica did, too. Only, he didn't know where she had disappeared to, and he had to find her before things blew up. Then I started nosing around, talking about Monica and some occult connection. More trouble.

When I came up with the address from Melvin, 227 B Street, it must have been a hell of a shock to him. He could stall me for a while, but sooner or later I'd find out the FBI connection, and then everything would start to unravel. So, exit Jason Coulter.

Of course, he couldn't just kill me, flat out. I'd made too much noise to other people about Monica and Roger. If I ended up mysteriously dead in my cabin, some of those others might start taking a serious interest. They just might locate Monica before he did. But if I had ended up babbling in a mental ward from the PCP, or better still, just driven off the canyon road, everything would work out fine.

Or, if I'd showed up dead in the empty house, next to Debbie, with NIGGER LOVER written on the wall, that would confuse things enough to buy some more time, enough to find Monica. God knows why he tried to kill me with a baseball bat instead of a gun. Maybe it fit some other scheme he had. Maybe he just didn't want to risk the noise; gunshots bring cops and witnesses.

But why the two black kids in the park, then? Why not just quietly take care of Monica, since he'd obviously located her? That still didn't make any sense. One thing was clear, though—the only way I was going to get it straight was by doing what I started out to do. Find Monica.

When I reached the cabin I could hear Stony scuffling around downstairs chasing something, so I opened a can of tuna and called him. He came bounding up the stairs, holding a mouse gently in his mouth. It was squeaking desperately. He ran up to the plate of tuna and carefully deposited the mouse on the side of the plate, where it sat trembling. Stony started gobbling his food, keeping one eye on dessert.

He was just doing his job, but it was a little much. I grabbed him by the tail and pulled him away. He yelped at me indignantly and the mouse took off for the corner. It slipped behind the stove and Stony looked at me in disgust, then went back to his dinner.

"It's okay," I told him. "I'm sure you'll find him again."

IT WAS STILL SNOWING WHEN I WOKE UP. I drank coffee, staring out the window, and thought about calling Dave. What would I tell him, though? I didn't have any hard evidence at all. He already thought I was halfway round the bend, what with all the occult crap I'd been pushing on him, and he wouldn't be too receptive to another far-out scenario. I needed Monica. Besides, it was a personal thing now. I didn't much care for having been played for a total fool.

This time at least I had a real lead on Monica, not something spoon-fed to me by Tony. I threw on a parka and some boots, and trudged down the road to my car. The snow let up by the time I passed Snowbird, and the valley was clear. A typical Alta snowstorm, clouds hanging right over the top of the canyon, and not much anywhere else.

By noon I was down at the Fred Meyer store on Thirty-third South. Linda, the pharmacist there, was a lady I'd met way back when I was working forged prescription cases.

"Jason!" she greeted me. "Where you been keeping yourself?"

"Oh, around. You?"

"Same old, same old. Working and playing."

"How's Cheryl?" Cheryl was Linda's big red chow that once tried to take a chunk out of my leg when I was visiting late one evening.

"She's fine. Still hates men."

"And yourself?"

"Oh, you know me. I can take 'em or leave 'em."

"Ah, yes, I do seem to remember something like that. Listen, Linda, I've got a little problem." I pulled out the bottle of codeine and placed it on the counter.

"Where did you get that?"

"The question is, where did it come from?" I placed my thumb by the sticker on the side. "Any idea what these numbers mean?"

Linda picked the bottle up and examined it. "Not one of ours. Looks more like a wholesale distributor's code."

"Any way of telling which one?"

"There are only two big ones in Salt Lake, Brunswick and Afton Pharmaceuticals. Brunswick is the biggest. They're over on Ninth South and Redwood Road. Maybe they can help you."

"Maybe they can," I said.

"Hey, drop over one of these days, why don't you? I'll lock Cheryl in the basement."

"It's a deal," I said.

BRUNSWICK DRUG WAS SECURITY CONscious. I had to be buzzed through the front door into the lobby, and the receptionist was behind the same kind of booth as the one at the FBI. She regarded me suspiciously, not inclined to help. I showed her my PI license, but it didn't cut any ice. Too bad Tony's FBI badge wasn't available.

She did finally agree to call a supervisor, and luck was with me. The supervisor was a small black woman with a neat Afro, and when I explained that the matter had a bearing on the murder of the two black joggers, protocol went out the window. She buzzed me through the second door and took the bottle from my hand.

"It's one of ours, all right," she said, holding it up. "Let's see what we can find out."

She led the way into a large room and walked over to a man seated in front of a computer. She put her hand on his shoulder.

"Bill, can you tell me where we shipped this?" she asked.

He looked up and read the code on the side of the bottle. "Probably. We don't get a lot of calls for codeine phosphate. Something like Percodan, we ship a hundred bottles a week." He pointed to the code. "09, that's September, 0500 is the lot number, 4221 is codeine phosphate. The writing was done by someone at the pharmacy it went to." He turned back to the computer and punched in some numbers. "I'll run a printout of the stores that were shipped a hundred lots in September."

In a few moments a printer across the room started clacking. I followed him across the room and bent over the printout. Several other employees came over, interested.

"Osco on Wasatch," he read, bending over the printout. "Pete's Pharmacy in Logan. M & M Pharmacy in Murray. Southeast Pharmacy, Salt Lake. Harvey's in Provo—"

"Harvey's?" interrupted a long-haired guy standing next to me. "Didn't one of the drivers say something about Harvey's last week?"

"Yeah, right," said another. "They were held up last month. Some guy in a ski mask, wasn't it?"

Bingo.

"Is that going to help you any?" asked the black lady.

"I certainly hope so," I said.

PROVO IS ONLY THIRTY-FIVE MILES SOUTH of Salt Lake City, but it might as well be in a different country. When you pull into town off the freeway, it's instant archetypal small-town America. The main street through town is Center Street—no one ever accused the Mormons of having overactive imaginations. A tree-lined center median runs down the middle of the street. The stores that line both sides are classic Middle America— Woolworth, Penney, a Paramount theater. All the faces are white.

It's a beautiful town, nestled right up against the base of the tail end of the Wasatch Mountains. You can almost see the clean air whistling off the mountaintops, and the purple hills crowd in so closely you're always conscious of them out of the corner of your eye.

But if Salt Lake City is bland, Provo is sterile. Compared to Provo, Salt Lake is a veritable Sodom and Gomorrah. Salt Lake at least tries for an occasional cosmopolitan fling; Provo flaunts its small-town smugness. The population is ninety percent Mormon, strict Mormon, and you feel guilty ordering a cup of coffee, much less lighting up a cigarette. The nearby Brigham Young University campus dominates the town, and the last student controversy at BYU was over whether to allow MTV to be piped into student housing. Needless to say, MTV lost.

The police station is a modern-looking affair in the middle of what passes for downtown. The first thing you see when you walk in is a huge candy machine. The next thing is a soda machine. If you successfully run that gauntlet you reach the information desk.

A young woman in a clerk's uniform was talking and laughing on the phone as I walked up. She let me wait while she finished her conversation, not hurrying, then looked up expectantly.

"I'd like to talk with someone in Robbery," I said.

She looked up at a name tag board on the wall. "Vern Thomas might be in." She got up, handed me a visitor's pass, and buzzed open the door leading back to the offices.

The detective division turned out to be a large room with six desks, five of them empty. Thomas was sitting at the sixth. He was a large round-faced man, slightly overweight, wearing a checked sport coat. He had *Mormon* written all over him. He didn't look much like a cop. On the other hand, some of the best cops look like insurance salesmen or ice cream wholesalers. I introduced myself and showed him my PI license. He glanced at it without any reaction. I guess my fame hadn't spread this far south.

"So, what can I do for you?" he said, pushing some papers off to the side of his desk.

I tried not to sprawl too casually in the chair across from him. I didn't light a cigarette.

"I'm working a case, looking for a missing girl up in Salt Lake. Word has it she might be with a guy who supposedly held up Harvey's Pharmacy here in Provo a few weeks ago. I was hoping you might have some idea of just who that might be."

"Harvey's?" Thomas looked at me blandly. "Well, we're working on it, checking out a few leads."

The standard line to civilians. "Any ideas you could share?"

He shook his head. "Not really. We're just checking out a few things. Just who is this girl you're looking for?"

"Her name's Monica Gasteau." I tried another tack. "If I could find her she might have something to say about the robbery."

"Gee, that's a thought," he said. "She might at that. Boy, I sure wish I could help you." No cop, even in Provo, is that naive. I was being royally put on. The small-town hick act. A look of friendly concern came over his face. "Tell me a little about this girl, why don't you?"

"Do me a favor," I said. "Call Dave Warren. He works Homicide up in Salt Lake."

"Sure, I know Dave," Thomas said. "He helped with the Farnsworth shooting a few years ago. Good man. Most of the city cops . . ." He trailed off. "Jason Coulter. Of course. That's who you are."

"I'm afraid so."

"You belong out at the Point," he said.

"Quite possibly," I said with resignation.

He unbuttoned his coat, settled himself a little more comfortably behind his desk, and studied me carefully. Now that he had relaxed I could see the sardonic gleam of intelligent humor in his eyes that I had totally missed before.

"You want to tell me what this is really about?" he asked.

I couldn't think of anything he would buy, so I told him the truth, or at least a part of it.

"Those two black kids up in Salt Lake, the ones who were shot? This Monica was a girlfriend, and I think she knows who killed them. Only, she's hiding out. The only lead I've got is some drugs that came out of the Harvey's robbery and turned up in Salt Lake. I think there's a connection between her and the guy who hit the pharmacy."

"You think he killed those two kids?"

I shook my head. "I just think he might know where she is."

"Uh-huh. And why is it you looking for this girl instead of the cops?"

I shrugged. "They've got their own agenda. They don't think she has anything to do with anything."

"But you know better, right?"

Thomas wasn't going to give me anything. I sighed and got to my feet. "Yeah," I said. "Unfortunately, I do."

He waited until I was almost out the door.

"Hold on a minute," he said. He pulled open the top drawer of the desk and took out a slim folder. "You know, if you're really on to something, which I doubt, I wouldn't mind seeing Salt Lake City with egg on their face for once. If not, it can't hurt anything to show you this." He smiled blandly and opened the folder. "Harvey's Pharmacy," he read. "Aggravated Robbery, September twelve, eight-thirty P.M. Suspect, MWA, six two to six four, muscular, wearing a red ski mask. Brandished a small handgun, pharmacist can't say what kind. No shots fired. Demanded Dilaudid, pharmacist doesn't keep it on hand anymore. Took a lot of class two narcotics, Percodan, Tylox, Demerol, a bunch of other stuff. Also cleaned out the till. No vehicle seen. No other witnesses."

He put the file back into the desk drawer and closed it gently as I walked back to his desk.

"That's it?"

"That's the basics. Not a whole lot to go on." Thomas leaned back farther in his chair, adjusted his jacket, and smiled. "Of course, that's just what's in the report." He sat there smiling, waiting for me to ask. I obliged.

"What else?"

"Well, nothing much really—except that I do know who hit the place. Can't prove it, but I know. I've got a couple of first-rate snitches."

"I'll be damned. Somebody local?"

He smiled again, affable. "Well, as a matter of fact, no. One of your boys up in Salt Lake." He paused about five seconds, enjoying drawing it out, before he spoke again. "Runs with the Pharaohs, I believe—name of Willie Waggoner."

I should have known. God damn.

"You know him?" Thomas asked, seeing the expression on my face.

"I know him. Shit. Of course. Badger Willie."

WHEN I GOT BACK TO SALT LAKE I STOPPED by Colson Insurance and talked to Brenda. She was a little doubtful, but gave me Badger's address anyway.

Badger lived on Pugsly street, in a large, run-down, two-story house. I pulled up across the street, noticing the three choppers parked in the driveway. Not good. The Badger had company. I lit a cigarette and leaned back in the seat. This was going to take some thought.

How to find out if Monica was in the house? I could just wait, but she might not come out for quite a while. Mean-

164

while, Badger with his biker paranoia, was bound to notice me sitting there.

Explain the situation to him? With the Badger, rational discourse was not a viable option. Badger was the type who didn't give a shit about anything or anyone, himself included. It was amazing he was still alive.

He wasn't going to scare, either. A lot of people think they're tough, but not many of them can look down the barrel of a gun without having their mouth dry up and their knees feel weak. The Badger was one of them. So, talk was out and force wouldn't work. That left the old standbys—deceit and trickery.

I didn't want to go in, not with a house full of bikers. So they had to come out. I remembered back when I was a young and foolish rookie cop, proud and honored to be on the SWAT team. After a particularly scary operation flushing a suspect from an abandoned house, the guy we caught critiqued our entire operation, tearing it apart with something like professional detachment. He had some good points. Finally I asked him how *he* would have got someone out of the house.

"Nothing to it," he said. "I would have set fire to the place."

Simple and direct. Of course, I couldn't burn down the house, but the principle was sound. I smoked another cigarette and let a few thoughts roam around.

I checked the back of the car. Some rags and an ancient stained roll of paper towels. I shredded the towels and tore the rags into thin enough strips to fit in my gas tank. After I dipped the rags in gasoline I gathered the whole mess and dumped it under the Harleys in the driveway. A book of matches made a nice torch, and I flipped them into the pile.

I ran up to the front door of the house and started hammering and hollering as loud as I could. The door was flung open by a very large and very pissed Badger, ready to pound something or somebody into the pavement. Then he saw his beloved chopper awash in flames. I ceased to exist and he brushed me aside with a swipe of one meaty arm. I could see two other bikers still inside, so I yelled at them, "Hey, man, your bike's on fire!" I stepped aside like a bull-fighter as they charged through the doorway.

I slipped quietly inside and looked around. A young, dark-haired girl came out from the hallway to see what all the commotion was about. She looked at me blankly. Of course, she hadn't the slightest idea who I was, but I somehow thought she should have at least said hello. After all, she had been a very important part of my life for quite a while now.

Monica.

13

"Monica," I said. She regarded me warily and I tried to reassure her. "It's okay, I'm a friend of Debbie's." She took a step backward and opened her mouth, about to yell for Badger. Once again I hadn't thought things through.

"The Badger," I said, improvising frantically. "He made a deal. Tony got to him. He's going to turn you."

That got to her. She closed her mouth. She didn't know who I was, but she knew Tony and she knew the Badger. What I'd said was more than possible.

"Who are you?" she asked.

Before I could answer, Badger came storming back in. The fire hadn't lasted as long as I thought it would. Another miscalculation.

I turned around just in time to have Badger grab me by the throat. He was a lot bigger than I was, and a hell of a lot stronger.

"Who the fuck are you?" he demanded.

I don't think he was really expecting an answer, since I obviously couldn't breathe, much less talk. It was more like a ritualized series of noises he felt obligated to make just prior to removing my head.

"Willie, don't! That's my brother!" Monica shouted.

He looked at her thoughtfully, trying to decide whether or not that particular bit of information was relevant. He must have decided it was, since he let go of my throat.

I tried to get his mind off what I was doing there. "Your chopper," I croaked. "Some guy torched it, just as I walked up. A real tall skinny dude. Bald, big mustache."

My description was a perfect match for one of the more distinctive members of the SoKos, the rival bike club in town.

"Chatley!" Badger said bitterly. "That cocksucking weasel. Fuck, but he's gonna pay."

I had a momentary twinge over possibly starting a biker war. Oh, well. I had other things to worry about. I rubbed my throat and looked over at Monica.

"Dad's real sick," I said. "He's at Holy Cross. They don't know if he's going to make it. I know you and him don't get along too well, but he'd like to see you before it's over."

The Badger looked at me with real concern on his face. "Hey, sorry, dude, I didn't know. What's wrong with him?"

"Heart," I said, thumping my chest.

"Oh. Too bad."

"Come on, kid," I said, getting to my feet. "Visiting hours end pretty soon."

Monica hesitated, making a decision. Finally she bought it.

"Just a sec," she said. "I gotta get my purse." She disappeared for a minute and came back carrying a small brown leather handbag. The Badger walked outside with us and stood by my car as we got in.

"Hope your dad's okay," he said.

Monica nodded and I pulled away. As we turned the corner I said, "That was pretty smart."

"How did Tony find out I was with Badger?" Monica asked, ignoring what I'd said.

"He didn't. I just said that to get you out of there."

Out of the corner of my eye I saw her hand reach out for the door handle.

"Don't jump out," I said. "Your mom hired me to find you."

She gave a short laugh. "My mom? My mom's the least of my problems."

She took her hand away from the door and rummaged around in her purse, pulling out a crumpled pack of Virginia Slims. She managed to ease one out that wasn't too bent, reached over, and punched the cigarette lighter in the dashboard. When she got the cigarette lit she took a quick drag, an unconscious parody of a movie tough street girl.

"So. Who are you anyway?"

"My name's Jason."

"What's this about Tony? You know him?"

"I know a lot of things. I found Roger. I found Debbie."

"You found Debbie? What do you mean, you found Debbie?"

"Debbie's dead. Tony got her, too."

She looked at me calmly. "What are you talking about?"

I pretended I hadn't heard her. "He's going to get you too, sooner or later. You want to play dumb, that's your choice. But if you want out, I can help you."

She stared out the window for a minute. The news of Debbie's death didn't seem to affect her much, but I could feel the wheels going around inside her head. She finally turned half sideways in the seat and put her hand lightly on my shoulder.

"Debbie's dead, huh?"

It was like she had shifted into another gear. A subtle change in body language, a slight alteration to the quality of her voice. An appealing, wistful vulnerability shining through her tough street kid veneer. Up to now I hadn't quite seen what all the fuss was about, but I was suddenly painfully aware of her presence next to me. She was seductive as hell. Not blatantly sexual, more restrained and innocent, hinting at passion just waiting to be awakened. Living, breathing kiddy porn.

"I've been scared," she said. She didn't look scared. Her next words came out hesitant and tremulous. "Will you really help me?"

"You bet."

"No cops," she said. "I don't have anywhere to go, though." She waited for an offer. When it wasn't forthcoming, she looked at me wide eyed. Her hand tightened almost imperceptibly on my shoulder. "Maybe I could stay with you until we figure out what to do?"

I didn't like that idea at all. A sixteen-year-old girl with a propensity for sexual blackmail was not my idea of the ideal houseguest. But I didn't dare let her out of my sight, and if I took her to the cops right now, there was no guarantee she wouldn't decide to play dumb. I needed enough time with her to figure out which buttons to push.

"Okay," I said, after some thought. "Just for tonight, though." A tiny self-satisfied smile appeared on her face. She figured she already knew which buttons to push, especially with men.

Monica was quiet as we drove down Wasatch Boulevard and reached the mouth of the canyon. I watched her out of the corner of my eye. She didn't ask about Debbie. She stared out the window humming to herself. It seemed she could adjust to new situations without a whole lot of thought or trouble. About halfway up, she said, "Gosh, it's pretty here," and fell silent again.

The clouds hung lower as we drove higher. Alta was still in the middle of its own private snowstorm when we pulled up next to the snowmobile. It had warmed up some, which made the snowflakes soft and huge.

"Next stage," I said, indicating the snowmobile.

I handed her my parka and she slipped it on. She climbed aboard behind me and wrapped her arms around my waist as we took off. As we roared up the road, she squealed with pleasure and hugged me tighter. She had left the parka unzipped and I could feel her small breasts pressing into my back. Like two kids, innocent and pure, whipping on a joyride through the snowy countryside.

When we entered the cabin she saw Stony and rushed over to pick him up. Stony took one look and dove for cover behind one of the big speakers. His intuitions were usually pretty good.

"You hungry?" I asked.

"Yeah, kinda," she said.

I dug some hamburger out of the fridge and some frozen French fries out of the freezer. Monica wandered around the cabin picking up things and putting them back down while I fried up the burgers.

"This is neat," she said, stopping by the window.

I brought the food over to the table where we could see out the window. It was getting dark and the snow was coming down even heavier. Monica was subdued, and I didn't push her about anything. After we finished she looked over at the big stone fireplace.

"Could we make a fire?" she asked, very polite and quiet.

"Sure," I said. "No problem."

I got the fire going and we sat in front of it, watching as the storm outside grew. After a while she leaned against me. I automatically put my arm around her and she sighed and leaned further into me. Two kids in front of a roaring fire, a mountain cabin, a storm outside. I luxuriated in the fantasy for about ten seconds, then straightened up, taking my arm away. I shook my head.

"Not with me," I said. "It doesn't work that way."

She wrapped her arms around her knees and gave me a knowing look. "But you want to, don't you?"

"That's not the point. It just doesn't work like that."

I thought she might get mad, but she just nodded and

moved a little farther away. I poked the fire, stirring it up a little.

"How did you get into all this, anyway?" I asked casually. "Roger and Tony and all?"

"God, who knows?" she said.

"Who'd you meet first?"

"Roger. He was always good for a place to crash, and he had real good dope."

She fell silent again. She didn't want to talk, but bit by bit I got the story. A lot of the girls on the street knew Roger. She started hanging around with him, mostly for the dope, then one day he introduced her to a guy who called himself Narada. She didn't know where Roger met him. Narada had a house up in the Avenues. One day, he and Roger told her they had started a church, the Church of the Four-Sided Triangle. A heavy dose of the occult, a heavier dose of drugs, and an even heavier dose of sex were the main tenets. A lot of the street girls got involved; there was always a good supply of drugs, and the occult angle seemed to turn them on. Debbie was one of the most enthusiastic converts. Monica just went along for kicks.

Then Roger found out who Narada really was. An FBI agent, what a kick. Roger smelled money and favors, so he came up with the idea of a photo session, with a big payoff to come. But he got the wrong kind of payoff.

"How did Tony let that happen?" I asked. "The photos? The guy's not dumb, you know."

"Roger had the camera hidden. We were supposed to split the money."

"But then he disappeared."

"Yeah. I knew what that meant, so I disappeared too for a while, went to L.A. Then I started thinking. Those pictures were still worth money. Maybe a lot. So I came back."

"You should have stayed there."

"I guess. Anyway, I came back and called Tony. I had it

all figured out. He was supposed to meet me in the park. With all those people around, what could he do? Besides, I told him Isaac would be with me and he knew all about it." She stopped and stared in the fire for a while. "I guess that wasn't such a good idea."

"No, I guess not. Did he?"

"Did he what?"

"Isaac. Did he know what was going on?"

She shook her head sadly. "No, he didn't know anything. I mean, he knew about the church and the sex and everything, but he didn't know about Tony. I just told him some guy was hassling me, and I wanted him along for protection."

"And Debbie?"

"She was more into all that stuff than I was. She didn't know who Tony really was, though."

I poked the fire some more. I could see it. Tony had the right idea. Get rid of both of them, Monica and Isaac. Make it look like a racial killing. But there were two black kids, and he didn't know which one was Isaac. So he shot both of them. By that time, he didn't really care.

Tony was the perfect textbook example of a sociopath. Most of them get away with it for years, and no one ever suspects a thing. What, Tony a killer? Good old Tony? No way. Outside, charming, friendly, very outgoing. Inside, something missing. Other people weren't very real to him. If the easiest way to solve a problem was to ignore it, fine. If the easiest thing was to kill someone, well, that was fine too. I was sure that if anyone looked closely at the time Tony was on the Dallas PD, they'd find a few unsolved homicides hanging around him. If you had to kill a few extra people to make sure everything turned out all right, so be it. And killing both black kids turned out to be an ironic bonus. Now it *really* looked like a racial thing.

The mistake he made was in shooting the boys first. He must have figured the girls would stand there in shock, and he could pick them off as well. But Monica fooled him; she was street smart. She started running after the first shot and didn't stop. He missed killing Debbie, too, but that didn't matter so much. She didn't know who he was. He'd have to deal with her eventually, just in case, but he had time. Nice of me to help him find her when she skipped from the hospital.

"Have you still got the pictures?" I asked.

Monica went over to her purse and rummaged through it. She pulled out two crumpled photos, started to hand them to me, then pulled back.

"These are kind of embarrassing, you know?"

"I know. I saw the others."

"Oh." She shrugged and handed them to me. They were pretty much the same as Roger's, a little more blurry. The main difference was that both faces were easily identifiable. I put them aside.

Tony had really screwed up, but with everyone in the city looking for a psycho racist, at least he'd bought himself some time. Things were holding steady. Then I showed up, not only looking for Monica but also for a guy who called himself Narada. A very unpleasant development.

He did pretty well, considering. He kept a close eye on what I was doing, working with me, guiding me away from danger spots, conning me into telling him how close I was getting. Meantime, maybe I could even help him find Monica.

"So, what do we do now?" Monica asked, breaking into my thoughts.

I didn't want to bring up going to the cops right off. So I started talking about the reward. She hadn't heard a thing about it.

"Ten thousand dollars?" she said, stunned.

"Maybe more."

"Wow. Really?"

"Really."

"Ten thousand dollars," she repeated. Going to the cops didn't seem to bother her so much anymore. She looked up at me shrewdly. "What's your cut?" she asked.

I didn't care much for her assumption I would want a

cut. Her instant acceptance of that as being obvious made me feel a bit sleazy. And of course she was right.

"Don't worry," I said. "We can deal with all that later."

She talked about what she was going to do with all that money, the clothes she would buy, the places she would go—maybe she'd even buy a used van. She never once mentioned Debbie or Isaac. Why should she? They were dead.

After a while she started yawning. I showed her which bedroom was hers, gave her one of my large turtlenecks for a nightgown, and left her downstairs. I was too keyed up for sleep, so I went back upstairs and settled back down by the fire, staring out the big front window.

The storm had picked up in intensity. The wind came in gusts shaking the cabin. The snow blotted out anything more than five feet outside the window. At times I couldn't even see the porch. It was easy to imagine the storm would go on forever, the snow falling and falling until the entire world was covered, like in the old Norse myths. Fimbul-winter, they called it, the last winter, the one that never ends. Those old Scandinavians had a grim worldview. Most cultures have a tradition of the battle between good and evil, but very few of them have evil triumphing in the end. The Norsemen did. Their gods knew it was hopeless—they were predestined to fail, but they fought on anyway. It wasn't the outcome; it was the fight that counted. It was a matter of integrity. They spent all their strength in a desperate attempt to hold back that inevitable fall of night. I understood them. What else can you do?

I got up and shoved another log on the fire. Stony came out cautiously from behind the speaker and sat on the hearth, ears straight up, staring out the window, keeping me company with the storm. I sat there until the fire burned down, gazing into the embers. I thought about Jennifer. I thought about Laura. I thought about a girl I hadn't seen in ten years. I thought about what I was doing with my life. After I'd thought enough, I slept.

14

I didn't sleep well that night. Every time I dozed off I dreamed Monica was creeping into my bed. We would start making love, and then I would notice she was holding something in her hand. I could never see what it was, and every time I tried to get a look she would somehow hide whatever it was, but I didn't have to see. I knew it was a knife. The sound of her closing the bathroom door finally woke me early in the morning.

We crossed paths as she came out of the bathroom. The shirt I had lent her barely came down over her hips, and she gave an exaggerated wiggle as she squeezed by. Only at sixteen can you look that good two minutes after you wake up.

I made some coffee and Monica insisted on cooking breakfast, bacon and eggs. I was a little dubious whether she could cook anything at all, but she did okay. We sat on opposite sides of the kitchen counter. I didn't say much, but she chattered on about various things, mostly money again. Stony sat in a corner and watched. He still didn't trust her.

The wind had died down some, but the snow had picked up, if anything, and the clouds were low enough to blot out everything except the nearest trees. There was close to twenty-four inches piled up on the porch. Down canyon I could see the snowplows clearing the parking lot. Too bad they didn't come up as far as the cabin.

I was thinking about what clothes I had for Monica suitable for the snowmobile when the front door burst inward. For a moment I thought there had been some sort of explosion, but a figure followed the door. It looked like a cross-country skier—hat and Smith goggles covered with snow, parka, windpants. The only incongruous note was the large-caliber automatic it held in its right hand.

The figure stood in the doorway for a moment, then stepped to the side, a little farther inside, and pulled off the ski hat. It was Tony, of course. I thought longingly of my Walther, carefully tucked away in the bed table drawer downstairs.

"Hell of a place to live," he said.

"Hell of a day to come calling," I said.

He stepped in a few more feet, looking around quickly, and motioned with the gun. "Away from the counter. Over by the window. One at a time. You first, Jase."

I got up slowly and did what he said. He stopped me after a few steps. "Turn around," he ordered. He must have sensed me tensing for a desperation spring. "Easy," he said. "Just checking for a gun."

I swung deliberately around in a circle, arms slightly outstretched. "Sit down," he said, satisfied. Monica joined me at the window table. Tony stood over by the fireplace. The cold air blew in through the open door.

"How did you know?" I asked.

He looked over at Monica. "Little Miss Greedy," he said. "She called me last night, late." I looked over at Monica and didn't say anything. "Twenty thousand. That's what she wanted to just go away and forget everything." He shook his head. "Some people just don't learn." He leaned carefully on the fireplace mantel and chuckled. "You know what she told me? A 'friend' had the photos and a letter that would get mailed if anything happened to her. She's not that smart. That one must have come from a TV show." I glanced at Monica again, but there wasn't anything to say. "Of course, it's a toll call from Alta to Salt Lake. I got the number she was calling from this morning."

"And now you're here."

"And now I'm here."

"And now what?" There was a moment's silence. "Yeah, I guess that's a stupid question," I said.

I thought about giving him the "You'll never get away with it" speech. He just might, though. A call to Dave later in the day—"Dave, I'm worried about Jase. I can't get hold of him. He called me last night, said he'd busted the case open." Occult Satan worshipers. Organized white supremacists. Tony would come up with something. They'd find me dead. Monica would be nowhere to be found. He just might pull it off.

"Doesn't it bother you even a little to kill so many people?" I asked, just to keep the conversation going. As long as he was talking, he wouldn't be shooting.

"You do what you have to," he said, without much inflection. It was curious. That's just what I always used to say. What goes around comes around.

"Sure," I said.

"Hey, none of this had to happen." He shook his head. "I like you, Jase, I do." I believed him. It wouldn't do me any good, though. He motioned with the barrel of the automatic toward Monica. "She's the one who screwed it all up."

"Right. It's all her fault."

"Her and that asshole Dodgson. Why couldn't they leave well enough alone?"

"Well," I said, "you know how people are." Tony didn't answer. I tried to keep the conversation going. "How are you going to explain this one away?"

"I'll manage," he said. His breathing started to speed up, breath coming in short, quick pants. It was a bad sign; it meant he was about to start the execution. I shifted my weight in the chair, ready to spring across the room. I'd never reach him, but it was better than sitting there obligingly, quietly dying.

Before I could move, Monica made a break for the stairway leading downstairs. I think she knew she wasn't going to make it, but she'd made the same decision I had. Tony took two quick steps toward the stairway and fired twice before she had taken more than a step. One round caught her in the back of the head and she pitched forward onto the floor. I think the other one missed, but it didn't make any difference.

The instant Monica jumped to her feet I threw myself out of the chair in the opposite direction, scrambling toward the open door. Tony twisted a quarter turn and took a step forward. I knew I wasn't going to make it either. As I lunged for the door I heard an outraged squall, and Tony stumbled as he fired. A small hole appeared in the middle of one of the Klipsch speakers.

The minute Tony fired at Monica, Stony had bolted from his corner. Tony stepped square on him, and Stony twisted under his feet, almost sending him down. Tony got a second shot off as I rolled through the doorway. I didn't feel anything, so I figured he had missed with that one, too. I slithered down the stairs without trying to get to my feet, sliding in the snow. Before I reached bottom I made my decision. Up, not down. The road leading down from the cabin was bare of cover and uninviting. Directly above the cabin was a stand of trees which would provide some shelter. If I could get into them, I had a chance.

The snow was coming down hard enough to cut any visibility past thirty yards. If I could get a lead, I could lose him. I knew the terrain and I was bound to be in better shape than he was. I'd been at the cabin all summer and was acclimated. Tony was a flatlander, and at nine thousand or so feet, that made a difference.

I hit the bottom of the stairs and scurried around the side of the cabin, out of the line of fire. Then I straightened up and zigzagged until I reached the first trees. I got behind one of them just as Tony rounded the corner of the building. He didn't waste time on another shot. He took off after me.

The snow level under the trees wasn't quite as deep as the unprotected slope, but there was still a good fifteen inches of fresh powder there. To make it worse, the frozen crust from the last storm lay underneath, making it difficult for me to keep my feet, and I couldn't afford to fall. On top of that I was wearing a light shirt, and my "shoes" were only socks. I was rapidly losing the feeling in my feet.

I plunged up the slope, scrambling and slipping, on all fours half the time, angling from one thick stand of trees to the next. Running uphill through heavy snow at high altitude is a cardiovascular nightmare. In less than a minute I was gasping like a drowning man. The only consolation was that I could hear Tony behind me, sounding worse.

I had only gotten about twenty yards ahead of him, but the trees and the sheet of falling snow made it difficult for him to get a clear shot. He stopped for a moment and cranked off a couple of rounds, but they weren't even close, and it gave me a chance to increase the distance between us.

I came out of the first stand of trees and stopped for a second, sucking huge breaths of air into my lungs. Thirty yards above, a second stand started, much larger, continuing up the mountainside. Between the two stands was an open slope, angling steeply upward. Once I made it through the open space I'd be home free.

I started up the slope. The snow was deeper, and my legs plunged in up to my thighs. The first ten yards weren't so bad, but then fatigue started to catch up with me. I tried to breathe in a rhythm, like a runner or cross-country skier, but my lungs were burning. Too many cigarettes. I'd always figured cigarettes would be the death of me one day, but this wasn't exactly how I had envisioned it. My legs were dead, starting to tremble with each step.

I made a supreme effort. The ground crust under the fresh powder was slicker than ever. I could no longer feel my feet at all and couldn't get any purchase in the snow. The slope steepened until I was floundering, almost swimming uphill. Five yards from the cover of the trees above, my feet went out from under me and I slid back halfway down the slope. I managed to stop my slide just as Tony came out from the cover of the trees below. I sprawled there, dark against the white snow, stretched out, a perfect target.

I thought about getting to my feet for one last effort, but it didn't seem worth it. I thought of Jennifer. I wished I had called her when I'd had the chance. Now she'd always wonder. I flashed on Laura and the Tarot reading I'd taken so lightly. Ten of Swords. Death. Ruin. Disaster. The failure of all plans. The ending of all hopes.

Tony stood there catching his breath. For a moment I thought he was going to say something, but he just raised the gun and leveled it at me. He steadied it, left hand supporting right wrist, the classic shooter's pose.

Just before he fired, I launched myself headfirst down the hill. It was steep enough to pick up speed quickly and as I skidded toward him, twisting and spinning, plumes of fresh powder spewed up from my path. I could hardly see him through it, which meant he could hardly see me. I could hear him firing, not quick, trying to be accurate. It's hard to hit a moving target with a handgun, though, especially when you can't see too well and sheer fatigue is making your hand shake. About fifteen feet from him, I gathered myself and came up off the snow. My momentum carried me through the air and I was on him before he realized it.

But he did have time to get off a final shot, and at a range of three feet it's hard to miss.

He shot low, and the bullet caught me in the left thigh. I'd been injured before—had even broken both wrists once falling backward on a basketball court—but this was the first time I'd been shot. The pain was like nothing I'd ever felt before. I'd been told that the shock of the bullet numbs you, but it didn't numb me. It was like someone had taken a twenty-five-pound sledgehammer, filed one side down to a fine point, and then hit me in the thigh with it as hard as they possibly could.

We both tumbled over and slammed up against a spruce tree, but Tony kept his hold on the gun. I knew the chances of getting it away from him were slim, so I didn't try. Before he could twist it around, I had hold of his hair with both hands and slammed his head into the tree trunk. He grunted but still held on to the gun. He was trying to bring it around to bear on me, but after his head went into the tree he was having trouble making his arms work properly. I pulled his head back and slammed it into the tree again. Then again. And again. And again.

The rough bark cut his head, which started to bleed. The blood made my hands slippery, but I didn't stop. At some point the gun had slipped out of his hands, but I didn't notice. What made me stop was when I noticed the sound his head made going into the tree had changed from a dull thud to a mushy plop.

I rolled off him and lay in the snow, gasping. My leg hurt like hell. I didn't even think of trying to stand up. Blood was spurting from the leg with each heartbeat, and the beats were rapid. I tried to staunch the flow of blood with direct pressure from my hands, but the blood just oozed through my fingers.

If I didn't move soon I was going to bleed to death right there. Me and Tony, partners to the end. That seemed like it would be a terrible shame after all the trouble I had been through, so I started to crawl.

Getting back down to the cabin wasn't so bad, except for the pain, because I could half slide through the snow, but getting up the stairs was another matter. I sat at the bottom of the steps to gather my strength until I realized I didn't have any strength left to gather. Things were already starting to take on a dreamlike quality. The only reality was the pain in my leg, throbbing and expanding until it was the focus of my universe.

I hitched one step up and the pain doubled. Another step and it doubled again. At this exponential rate, I should pass out on the fifth step. I pulled myself up another, then another. There was no thought in my mind. Just the pain and the crawling and the next stair.

After a while I realized I was inside. I didn't remember crawling through the door. I tried to remember where the phone was. On the counter, that was it. I crawled a while longer. Something got in my way, annoying me. I tried to crawl over it but I couldn't. It took a couple of minutes to figure out what it was. Monica, lying where she'd been shot. Poor Monica. I tried to pat her gently, but missed. I wondered what I could do for her. Nothing. But wasn't there something else I had to do? The phone. Of course. But it was up on the counter, far, far away. How to get there? Far too high for me to climb. Ahh, the cord. I grabbed hold of the cord, very pleased with myself. I was a clever fellow, no doubt about it. But why was I holding the phone cord? Oh, yes, the phone. I gave it a feeble yank and it slid down off the counter, hitting me on the head with a jangling roar, turning things dark for a moment. Sad, Jase, very sad. Killed by a telephone. What a comedown for an old pro. I picked up the receiver off the floor and stared at the little buttons glowing at me. Who had I wanted to call? Jennifer, that was it. But I couldn't remember her number. I started to cry. Things got dark again and I started slipping away. The high-pitched beeping of a phone off the hook brought me back and I had a moment of lucidity. Pull yourself together, you asshole, I thought. You don't, you die. I depressed the button until I got a dial tone and carefully dialed 911. A voice materialized magically on the other end of the line.

"Nine-eleven emergency services."

"This is an emergency," I said painstakingly. "I've been shot. My name is Jason Coulter, and I'm in a cabin at Alta."

At least, that's what I thought I said. What actually came out was an inarticulate gurgle.

"I'm sorry, sir, I can't quite hear you," the operator said.

I gurgled again. The operator's tone became sharp and peremptory. "Sir! *Don't hang up the phone!* If you can hear me, try to speak, but *don't hang up the phone!*"

I tried to speak but couldn't. I suddenly felt unutterably weary. The receiver slipped out of my hand, and I slowly pitched face forward on the floor. A small, furry face appeared in my line of vision. Who's going to take care of Stony, I thought. Then it all turned gray. Then it all turned black.

EPILOGUE

It took seven months before my leg fully recovered. It still fatigues easily and hurts when I'm tired. But I'm lucky to even be here at all—the femur was shattered and the femoral artery severed. That's really what saved me, that and the cold. The artery went into spasm and kept me from bleeding out. Even so, they had to pump five units of blood into me when I reached the hospital.

The 911 operator locked my call and the Alta marshal's office told them where the cabin was. They said the chopper pilot from LifeFlight was amazing. The clouds were so low he couldn't see anything for the last couple of miles, so he hopped from treetop to treetop, hovering, waiting for little breaks in visibility.

Laura came to see me twice at the hospital. The second time she brought her ex-husband with her, only he wasn't ex- anymore. They had decided to give it one more try.

I did get the reward money. Most of it went for medical bills and the rest for living expenses. As for Monica's parents, I could hardly send them a bill under the circumstances. They took her death pretty hard, especially her father.

I never did call Jennifer.

I ran into Melvin on the street one day. He just looked at me and said, "What'd I tell you?"

He had me. All I could do was nod knowingly and say, "FBI, man. FBI."